NEED (FETTERED #7)

Ari & Jackson

LILIA MOON

COPYRIGHT

DON'T MISS BOOKS!

It's Ari here, people. Pay attention, because I want to make sure you make it to my new series...

Lilia's really sweet, so she's giving you choices. Pick the one that works best for you (and do pick one—this is the final *Fettered* book and we don't want to lose you!)

1. **Preorder.** There's a link to the first book of the awesome new *Handcrafted* trilogy at the end of this book, or here, if you're impatient like me. *Twisted Strands* is fantastic. Cute kittens, hot canoe sex, and Fettered's best ropes guy. You totally want to read it. (My new series comes later. We have a little work to do before we're ready for you.)

2. **Email List.** There are two. One sends you a notification for each new series, one lets you know about every new book. I wanted an extra one with bonus spankings, but somehow that hasn't happened yet. Click here to sign up for the list you prefer.

Now go read. I'll see you at the end. ;)

xo Ari

Chapter One

ARI

I look down at Emily's footwear and manage my usual grin, because the shoes totally deserve it. They're red and *really* sparkly and a nice match for her very rosy cheeks. Her Dom must have been harassing her on the way in the door. "Nice shoes."

She clicks her heels together and laughs. "There's no place like home."

There isn't—and she does a lot these days to brighten mine. Which feels important tonight. I'm a little raw and I know it. I hold out the scanner to check her thumb in to the club and look into the empty space behind her. "What did you do with Damon?"

She shakes her head and looks amused. "He's outside taking a call from the *Dish*."

Their lifestyle blogger has fallen a teeny, tiny bit in love with Fettered and the man who owns it. "Everything okay?" Our first run-in with Mari Trilo was a little rough, but Emily doesn't look concerned. She shouldn't—she's done more to soften and shine our image in the city than anyone.

"She wants his input on a list of adventurous toys for your lover's stocking this Christmas."

This time my laughter doesn't take any effort at all. "And what bad thing did Damon do that you're making him take the call?"

Emily grins. "He's withholding spankings."

Foolish Dom. She's wearing her yellow sundress, the one that could visit any nice cafe in town. The one she wears when she really means business. "Tell me you've got something on underneath your dress that matches the shoes."

Her cheeks fire up again, but the rest of her looks very pleased with herself. "I'm not wearing anything underneath. Which I might have mentioned to Damon as we came up the walkway."

Sam, who scooted through the door in time to catch the last of that, hoots and wraps his arms around Emily from behind. "You go, sugar. Make him beg."

Leo growls meaningfully, which has exactly zero effect on Sam.

I shake my head, but this is exactly why I sit at the front door night after night and greet my people. "How's Soleil?"

Sam lets go of Emily and gives me a hug and a kiss too. "Sound asleep with Gabby and Daniel watching over her. They said we need to get out for the night."

Leo snorts. "No, they said *you* need to get out."

Sam, who's a brat, but not an idiot, melts into the Dom who adores him.

I look down at my tablet so they don't see what rises in my eyes. I don't hide, but I don't make my friends sad either. Not when they're exactly what I need.

The door opens again and Emily, Leo, and Sam take the hint and head into the lounge. Mattie blows in, holding the door as Milo joins her, looking like a wide-eyed newbie. Which means Sam isn't the only sub stirring up trouble tonight, although if I know Mattie, and I do, she's going to make her Dom wait for it.

Mattie casts me a quick, gleeful glance, one that stutters when she meets my eyes.

I shake my head just enough for her to see and Milo to miss. Not tonight—it's not sympathy I need. It's family.

She winks at me and spanks Milo's ass. "Gotta go, hot stuff. I promised Meghan I'd help her hand out drinks for a while."

I snort as she pushes through the door, shaking her scantily clad ass at her man. The subs are definitely on a roll this fine evening. I might have to join them. Being a brat fixes a lot of things.

Milo chuckles quietly and shakes his head. Then he gives me a slow, quiet once-over and holds out his arms. "Come here, you."

Damn. Sometimes I wish I worked with people who are a lot less observant. I slide into his arms anyhow. I've never walked away from hugs, especially ones from people who love me and know exactly when and why I hurt. "Sorry. I'm a little tender tonight. I spent the afternoon with Gabby and Daniel, and they're just so darn lit up on each other."

He doesn't say a word. He just kisses the top of my head and holds me tight.

I can feel the tears coming, and I don't want to let them arrive. Ever since Xander decided he was heading for the job in New York instead of here, something inside me has been standing a little too close to the waterworks tap. It needs to stop. I'm fine with having feelings, but I pride myself on living with two feet planted in the reality of what is, not in a romantic pipe dream I concocted out of nothing more than a couple of fun play sessions with a guy from L.A. who happened to really know his stuff.

"He isn't ready for you," says Milo quietly into my hair.

I don't want that to be true. "The man has mad skills."

"I know." A long pause, and another squeeze around my ribs. A friend who knows exactly how to soothe me. "You need more than that. He's a good guy, but he's not ready to get as naked as he would need to get with you. Or as soft."

I push away, instantly pissed off and scared and fine with letting him see both. "Don't put me up on a pedestal. I'm not some goddess of love and kink no guy could possibly handle."

He reaches out and touches my cheek. "That's exactly what you're afraid you are."

Fuck. I know better than to speak before I think, especially when this particular Dom is paying attention. "I have a fat head, huh?"

He chuckles. "The whole time I've known you."

I make a face and punch his bicep. "Go. Stop loitering in my foyer. I have people to let in." I wait until his hand reaches the inner door. "And thank Mattie for sharing you."

He doesn't object to the term, even though the two of them are absolutely, adorably exclusive. He knows what I mean. That spank on his ass when she headed into the lounge was my soul sister sending her very best person to act as temporary stand-in for what I really want.

I sigh into my suddenly quiet foyer. This is not a rut I want to be in. I know I live a charmed life. Milo is only one of the many amazing people in my world who see me and know me and take care of my heart every day. But even a brief hug from a man who wants to protect me from the world is an aching reminder.

I have so many Doms who love me. But none of them are mine.

Chapter Two
JACKSON

Scorpio fades out the last notes of the song we just finished and turns off her mike. Break time. The night is young yet, but she's good at feeling out the moods of the crowd. Tonight they're still mellow, happy to chat while the entertainment takes a little down time.

She leans her guitar against Eli's keyboard and gives me a look. "Nice beat you had going on that last one."

I know that tone. She's not over here to talk about my drumming skills. "Thanks."

She glances casually at Quint, who's messing with the new guitar string that keeps sliding infinitesimally out of tune and driving him nuts. "We can take a longer break if you want. Give you a little time to go find a play buddy."

I wondered when she'd join that line-up. Scorpio isn't the queen of logistics because she's good at letting things happen at their own speed and time. "No, I'm good. I brought my hand drums in case you want to mess around with a ballad or two later."

Her eyes flick over to Quint again, and for a moment I

think that I've successfully managed to throw him under the
bus. Then the man with the perfectly tuned guitar looks up
and I see the tank behind the bus. "A longer break sounds
good. I'll go bartend with Meghan and man a playlist from
there for a while."

Eli's suddenly paying attention to this conversation too.
Which confirms what I had already figured out.

My band is staging an intervention.

Eli points a wry smile my way. "You could do a groupie or
two a favor and save them from Chloe's wrath."

Chloe has some very scary looks, especially for a sub.
They're all for show, because she also has the high-octane self-
assurance of a woman who knows she doesn't need to do
anything more to keep her Dom than breathe. Personally, I
think she toys with the groupies occasionally just to make Eli
squirm, but I'm smart enough to keep that thought to myself.
Subs have some very inventive ways of getting even. "I don't
think a groupie is what I need tonight."

"Maybe not." Quint's voice is casual. The kind of casual he
used in training right before he lopped off some poor baby
Dom's head. "But you do need to stop being a tourist. You've
taken the training and you've got good instincts, but you don't
turn into a Dom by sitting on a stool."

I don't turn into the kind of Dom I want to be by fondling
random subs, either.

Scorpio doesn't say anything. She lets the two big tough
guys in the band do the talking, and then she levels me with
nothing more than a look. One that says I matter and I need
to spit out whatever I'm not saying before she brains me with
her guitar.

I sigh and get honest, because it's either that or play the
kinds of games I gave up in middle school. I know I matter to

all three of them, and one of the reasons I walked in the door of Fettered in the first place was to find a tribe that knew how to keep it real. "I'm not planning to scene with anyone tonight. I know you all think I should, and I know you've got reasons, but I have some as well. I'm asking you to respect my choices."

"We do." Quint pulls over Eli's stool and takes a seat. I can see eyes in the crowd watching us—the band doesn't usually take a break and then stay onstage. "But you're new here, and that comes with responsibilities for you and for us. Yours start with talking. You're a risk to yourself and others if you don't, which is a lecture I gave on the first day of class and you were one of the few smart enough to be listening, so don't make me say the rest of it again."

He's so very much like the man who taught me everything I know about playing the drums. Tough, dangerously insightful, and good all the way through.

Eli and Scorpio have taken up flanking positions in support of us both. And in quiet threat. Nobody pulls any of their punches around here.

I set down my drumsticks. I came here to be real. I remind myself that means something different inside these walls than it does out of them. "The woman I want to scene with—I can't give her what she needs yet."

His eyes widen. I've surprised the hell out of him, which any other day I'd be enjoying quite a bit.

He frowns at me. "Who?"

I don't say anything. I just look over at the door. The one that leads to the front foyer.

Quint follows my look and sucks in a breath. "Oh, hell."

Those two words hang in the air for another breath, and then he reaches for his guitar. "No ballads. Let's do something with a beat."

I pick up my sticks. What we play next won't change the message he just sent. The one that was all action and left no room for doubt.

He doesn't think I'm ready either.

Chapter Three

ARI

Kink is most of my life. Yoga is only a little corner, but it's a corner I work hard to make time for. Which is why I'm here, even though I had to pull leggings out of the laundry pile to do it.

I walk into the studio at Breathe, one of the very few places in town where nobody knows what I do with the rest of my life, and exhale into the serene vibe. Dreamy music underpins the murmurs of conversation and mats unrolling and people beginning to let go of their tight places in this oasis from the busy of their lives. Athena flutters her fingers at me from the front of the room. She's a tiny, stocky woman who looks nothing like a dancer until she starts to move, and she pulls in a full house for every single one of her classes, even at the ungodly hour of ten a.m.

I roll out a yoga mat and towel, which is fortunately cleaner than my leggings. It won't stay that way for long. This is hot yoga, which was invented thousands of years ago by the same person who invented kink, or least that's the theory I'm sticking with.

Athena shuts the studio door, the quiet clink of the gates

of hell closing. The two massive heaters in the room start spewing out hot, dry air, which will turn this place into a desert in about three more minutes.

Then we'll start sweating and turn it into a stinky rainforest.

I nod and smile at the two people wedged in on either side of me as we line up mat edges and peel off all the clothing that vanilla people consider acceptable to shed in public. We're about ten minutes away from being slimy together, which is a weird form of bonding with strangers when there hasn't been a limits conversation first. The guy to my right is a good person to be parked beside—he's got a really good sense of where his skin ends and the rest of the world begins. The woman on my left is still a little shy, but less than she was last week. She's new, but she's got moves when she's sweaty.

I laugh quietly at myself and wipe invisible lint off my mat. This isn't my club and Athena doesn't need me babysitting her newbies.

There's a disturbance in the force at the front of the room, and I lift my head to look. I can't see for a moment, and then enough bodies shift that I can see the trim lines and easy moves of the new arrival. Trim lines and easy moves I've seen before. The man dropping his bags gently on the floor and scanning the room is none other than Fettered's resident drummer.

I make a face, because Jackson doesn't look like he rolled out of bed and got dressed from his laundry pile, and yet I know for a fact that he left the club only a few minutes before I did last night.

The shy gypsy on my left leans over to get a better look and sighs happily. "Oh, wow. I didn't know he was going to be here."

I grin and wonder if Jackson knows he's got groupies everywhere. The ones at the club tend to send him into hiding.

Athena moves, and Jackson's eyes track her—and then along the line of sight beyond her straight to me.

I can see the surprise on his face. I smile and wave. I'm sure I'm far more used to running into club friends in the grocery-store aisle and the rest of life than he is. He'll get used to it. Some days, Seattle feels like a really small town.

I get a small smile back as he pulls a set of hand drums out of a hand-woven bag done in gorgeous, earthy colors that just want to be stroked. He folds the bag carefully, almost reverently, and sets it aside. A tool, then, and one he cherishes. He taps lightly on the top of one of the drums as he pulls a water bottle out of a different bag, one he treats far more casually.

As he sets his water down, he catches me still looking at him.

I see the surprise, and the pleasure. And a man who doesn't bother hiding either.

Interesting. He's a lot more buttoned down at the club.

Athena steps into the formal lines of mountain pose at the front of the class, her body signaling so that her words don't need to. She talks less than any yoga teacher I've ever known, which makes us all pay very close attention. I know some Doms who should take lessons.

She glances over at Jackson, who's set up a beat to help call the class to order, and nods, pleased. He does something fast and tricky with one hand that sounds a little bit like laughter and puts smiles on at least half the faces in the room.

Athena full-on grins at him and turns back to the class. "Ready to get hot and sweaty, people?"

She's not the ethereal Zen kind of yoga teacher.

There are a few moans and grunts as people make final

peace with choosing to torture themselves like this. The rest of us just glug water. We know what's coming.

I glance at Jackson, who's wearing a lot more clothes than most of us, and wonder what the heat and humid sweat will do to his drums. Then I look at the African print on his special bag and stop worrying.

His drums will revel in this.

I'll do my best not to want to kill them.

Chapter Four

JACKSON

She's beautiful.

I never get to watch her full-on like this without worrying about who might be watching me. Drummers are supposed to watch the people they drum for, and as an added bonus, at least half the yoga poses so far have demanded that Ari's head go somewhere that she can't catch me staring.

I wouldn't care, except I need time yet, and I'm not sure I'll get it if she figures out why my eyes are on her.

Fortunately, she's pretty thoroughly distracted. The room got African levels of hot about ten minutes ago, and the sheen of sweat on skin has taken us all to a place of earthy and tribal and primal. A jungle of carefully coordinated spandex. I grin. Kengali would laugh. He found white people hilarious in general, and me in particular. The earnestly sweaty people in this room had nothing on me when I showed up for my adventure in his little corner of Gambia. I'd gone to spend a year as a well-meaning student, hoping to use some of my privilege to bring change to somewhere that needed it.

Then I heard the drums and proceeded to spend six years letting them change me.

I let my fingers work the drum skin Kengali helped me stretch when he decided I'd finally sat still and listened long enough. It's not the most well-made of my drums, but it's the one most tolerant of being dragged around a cold, windy city. Its sound is changing as the room warms up. I run my eyes over my audience again, slowing the rhythm of my hands to match the stretchier pose Athena has just called for. I'm learning to recognize most of their names, even the Sanskrit versions. Like the names of most of the drum beats I learned, they sound far fancier in a language that isn't my own.

Athena makes a motion with her arms, and her students tip over into something that goes by the innocent name of triangle pose. About half of them make it. The other half grab various parts of their bodies and try not to die. I send them as much empathy as I can with my fingers. I know what it is to be the guy who doesn't bend the way everyone else does.

Ari bends, with grace and strength that makes it look like human beings were born to be triangular. It doesn't surprise me—she makes climbing onto a spanking bench look easy and graceful too. Which isn't something I've watched very often, but every time is seared in my memory.

I may not have told my band members the whole truth yet, but I've said it to myself. Six years in Africa and I've been looking for a home ever since—and something deep inside me thinks I might find it with the woman in a simple black tank top, arching over into a backbend on her way back up to her feet. Most of the rest of the class can barely untangle themselves from triangle pose the easy way.

My fingers tap her a message before the rest of me can get a grip. So beautiful. So freaking strong and bendy and amazing.

I swallow. She doesn't speak the language of drums. She won't know. But maybe the part of her soul where we're all born with a beat in our veins will hear anyhow.

One of the guys in the back row topples over into the equally inflexible, very sweaty guy beside him, and half their line goes down. Athena grins, leaves me at the front, and heads into the fray, dodging limbs and sweat puddles like a pro.

I make a face and free up one hand from the rhythm and drag my shirt over my head. Athena wasn't kidding about the temperature, and clearly the part of me that got used to hot-and-humid in the jungles of Gambia hasn't shown up yet this morning. My t-shirt is a sweaty mess, and unlike the poor people falling off their yoga mats, I'm just sitting comfortably in a corner.

I take another survey of the room, aware Athena is still untangling people at the back, and catch Ari staring.

Straight at my naked chest.

I've seen naked men before. Lots of them. More than most women will see in ten lifetimes.

And I can't take my eyes off him. It's not even his chest, sexy though it is. It's the utterly unselfconscious way he just peeled himself naked. The way he's holding the container for an entire class of uncomfortable people as they sweat out their crap and breathe in something better to replace it—and while he's doing all that he just reached up and pulled off his shirt without missing a beat.

He knows I'm looking. He knows, and he hasn't looked away or gotten shy or pumped up his muscles or done anything other than meet my eyes.

I don't misread people. It's one of my superpowers, knowing who someone is just by how they land in my foyer. But I've totally missed a whole bunch of layers of this man. He's as sweaty as we are—even his fingers are shiny. But he's the only one in this room besides Athena who isn't some degree of uncomfortable, who isn't having to fight his way into relationship with the heat that's pressing on our bodies of water, reforming us into differently shaped clay.

He's already been pressed.

I don't know how I know that, but I do. My superpowers, showing up several months late.

I narrowly miss getting clocked by the swinging arm of the guy on my right, which means I've missed whatever Athena just told us to do. I take a look at the scooping warrior poses all around me and hastily catch up. Then I go back to staring at Jackson's chest. At his face. At the hands that know so precisely what they're doing that he doesn't need to look at them.

I know this because he's looking at me.

Looking, and seeing, and he's not making the mistake of seeing the slightly uncomfortable sweaty blonde cheerleader. Kinky people are better at looking past surfaces than most, but he's just barely kinky, so new to my world that he's still wearing some of the crinkly packaging he came in.

But underneath that is a guy who just got interesting.

He's holding this room, and he's doing it so smoothly that Athena has ceded control without even realizing she's done it and the shy gypsy beside me has forgotten she's shy. That's a skill that can be taught, and I work really hard with Quint to teach it, but whatever else Jackson might need to learn before he isn't a baby Dom anymore, holding a container isn't it. He's woven himself into this room. Quiet, competent dominance, and it's sexy as fuck.

I manage to shift to the next pose without inconveniencing the guy beside me. I've lost track of Athena's words, but that's okay. My body knows how to do this—and if it forgets, there's a drumbeat telling me where to go. What to do. How to be right here in my sweaty skin and trust.

I swallow and bend over toward my toes, a waterfall of sweat running up my face for just long enough to have to run back down again when I stand up. I screw my eyes shut—my eyes have standards for the salty water they're willing to hang out with, and sweat doesn't cut it.

The drumbeat tells me to hold still just a minute longer, that there are rewards for hanging upside down and letting sweat run into my nose.

Which is such a completely, totally, utterly Dom thing to do, and it's doing things to my insides that just should not happen in yoga class. He makes me want his hands drumming on my ass or sliding into the wet heat of my pussy, showing me where to stay and where to go and when to do the thing I don't want to do to get to where I need to be.

I swallow and try to shift my attention back to whatever version of hell-baked warrior pose this is.

His drum laughs at me. Tempts me. Calls my blood to something it knew long before it met yoga.

I growl, which scares the shit out of the shy gypsy and nearly has her taking out half the row. I wince and make apologetic faces at all the eyes that turn my way.

I don't look at Jackson, not even when he does the laughing beat again. He's a freaking baby Dom and he's scening with me, right here, right now in the middle of four-dozen sweaty people who have no idea what they're part of, and we're going to dump all these innocent bystanders on their asses if we're not careful.

If *he's* not careful. I am so not the one who started this.

Chapter Six

JACKSON

I didn't mean to go here. Not yet. I know I'm not ready, and if I start this before I can finish it, she's not going to take me seriously enough for this to work.

I know all that. I've repeated it to myself over and over for months as I watch her work the floor at Fettered while I bang on my drums, and I'm saying it now as I watch her sweat to my beat. She's allowing herself to be taken over by it, which is a gift, because way too many people on this continent don't remember what their blood was born to do. They listen politely to my drumming. Ari's letting herself mate with it.

I breathe. I'm not ready. Kink is a skill, just like drumming, and I spent three years at the feet of the masters, just listening, before I got to touch my first hand drum. Kengali was hardcore that way, but those three years turned me from a white kid who thought he wanted to play the drums into a man who could feel the beat of my own soul.

If waiting three years to touch Ari is what I need to do, then it's damn well going to happen. But that doesn't mean I can't give her a taste of what lives inside me. I change up the rhythm a little, adding a slow, intricate sub-rhythm that eases the more attentive ears in the room slightly off center, invites them to step outside their comfort zone and stretch.

Ari is one of the first to notice. Her hand, reaching for the mat, goes entirely still. Listening. Waiting for the response that she knows will rise deep inside her.

A woman who knows, absolutely, how to trust.

I'm not ready yet. But I want, in every cell of me, to earn the right to that trust. For now, though, it's enough just to play at its edges. I blur the center rhythm a little. Not much—they're packed in here like really sweaty sardines, and one jagged beat would send half the room tipping over like dominoes.

Or so I like to think. You can't be a good drummer without some ego.

The woman beside Ari wavers, sucked in by the off-beat and not sure what to do about it. I flutter fingers on the edges of my drum, sending out reassurance, but not bringing the pulsing of my hands entirely back into alignment.

Athena raises an eyebrow. She might not know anything about drumming, but she can feel what I'm doing. Then she grins and ducks under an errant leg, laying her hands on the hip it's attached to. Offering steadying. Partnering with my drumbeat and letting it do whatever I have in mind.

I'm going to like working with her.

I look back over at Ari. There are three people in the room who've solidified into the new rhythm, and she's the strongest of them. It's contagious—her confidence is reaching two layers deep into the people around her. Someone who builds tribe, leads it, even when she's got sweat dripping off her nose.

I know all this already. She's strong and generous and wide open and she somehow calls people in past the gorgeous exterior and lets them see all that. She's amazing. But today, I'm seeing something I didn't know, because she's leaning into the beat I'm offering her and for the first time that's allowing me to see something else.

Her longing.

I swallow and start to gentle my hands. I don't want to. I want to take her deeper, to go where my hands and her soul both want to go right now. I can feel the confidence in my beat. *Ready. Ready.*

But I can't.

Because I'm holding forty-six people in this room, not just one.

Because my head isn't nearly as convinced as my hands.

Because Ari is already firming back up.

But she let me see something in these few sweaty minutes, and it's changed the whole story I've been telling myself for months. This isn't just about me—it's also about her. About something way down deep she just let my drum touch. Something raw and human and needy and urgent and real.

Something that says I haven't got three years.

Chapter Seven

ARI

I set another pile of gear on the floor beside Mattie and take a seat. Doms usually take good care of their personal stuff, but the club gear sometimes gets cracked or dusty or dangerous in subtle ways that need experienced eyes to find them.

I do it because it's my job. Mattie does it because a decent number of these tools have been used on her ass, so she's paying it forward. And because I brought chocolate. A whole plate of stupendously decadent orange-spice dark-chocolate truffles. They're basically a food orgasm, but every time I suggest that for the packaging, the cute couple in their fifties who make them just blush and pat me on the head.

The truffles are shaped like bears today, which makes me feel oddly carnivorous as I bite off a head. "You want crops or paddles?"

Mattie grins. "Paddles. I like oiling the wood."

And hiding the mean ones at the very back of the cupboard, but we'll both pretend I don't know about that. I'm a switch when I'm actually playing, and I pull out my Domme voice when I have to, but the rest of the time I live in the skin of a club brat. Submissive with just enough tricks in her pocket to keep people on their toes.

I pick up the crop on the top of the pile and start wiping it down, checking stitching as I go. Quint will be using these for a training class next week, and we have standards to maintain. I pull out the less bendy ones with the big leather ends out first. The small, whippy ones aren't for beginners, even beginners Quint has deemed worthy of touching a crop.

Mattie hums under her breath, a totally different song than the one playing over the sound system. And says nothing, which isn't like her at all. I raise an eyebrow. "What's on your mind?"

She grins. "Nice try. Talk."

I offered her chocolate bribes to do toy maintenance with me long before I had anything to talk about, but she always knows. "If Milo hadn't come into the picture, do you think you could have paired off with a baby Dom and made it work?"

Her oiling cloth freezes in mid-air. "Seriously? Who?"

So much for leading questions and hypothetical discussions that might not make me squirm. I sigh and reach for another crop. They're all in good working order, which isn't giving my squirmies anything to keep them busy. "Jackson."

Her eyes widen. "Sexy drummer Jackson?"

I shrug and rub my fingernail over a fraying thread that isn't fraying. "Yup. Sexy. Also, baby Dom." That's enough shorthand for her to know exactly where my head's at, even if the rest of me is finding it a lot harder to get in line with where that story ends.

She eyes me carefully. "He's interested?"

Very, although I can't believe how long he kept it under wraps. I've been the object of a lot of trainee crushes, and I always know. Which makes me wonder if this is something else. If *he's* something else. I sigh. That's really dangerous ground, and it lives in the most tender area of my heart. Lands that just recently got stomped on by a sexy Dom from L.A. with skills Jackson won't have for years yet.

Mattie's watching me with a mix of alarm and compassion, not even pretending to oil her paddle anymore. "Are *you* interested?"

My fingers wrap more tightly around a crop handle, trying to find the answers my body doesn't have. "I'm not sure. And even if I am, I'm not sure I want to be."

She laughs quietly. "That's not how it works, girlfriend. You know that."

I do. Which is why I'm sitting here with the kind of uncertainty in my belly that I usually walk other people through. "He showed up at my yoga class this morning with a hand drum and quietly owned the room."

Mattie's head tips down, but I don't miss the flash of delight in her eyes.

I sigh. Everyone here has been drinking from the same damn fountain of pink-Koolaid love. "Baby Dom, Mattie. Really baby. Like Quint only kicked him out of trainee class a few weeks ago level of green."

She looks back up, and the delight is gone. "You think he can't hold you."

"Most can't." It's not arrogance making me say that, it's truth. Truth, and pure, needy frustration. I've spent my whole adult life walking the journey into all of who I can be—and I've turned myself into someone most guys don't know how to handle.

"I know." Her voice is quiet, but her empathy fills every crevice of the hallway.

I let the rest out, because even though we both know it, I need to say it. "I play hard. I need to be pushed, and I need someone who won't fold at my experience or my self-confidence or because I know more than they do about pretty much everything kinky."

Not to mention being a switch. Which is really great for playing the field and really sucky for trying to leave it.

Mattie leans forward and rests her forehead on mine. "Tank and Eva are getting there."

Tank is a really rare find. And even though Eva's a sub with a lot of experience, her needs are a whole lot simpler than mine. I laugh, because they're a whole lot louder too. "She just wants to be spanked and make lots of noise."

Mattie giggles. "She's really good at it."

She is, and Tank's finally got that all the way figured out, which is even funnier. I love the two of them together—I just don't think they're me. And with all of the other examples at the club where one person is new, and they are freaking legion lately, it's the sub who's green.

Baby Doms are a whole different ballgame.

Chapter Eight

JACKSON

Quint notices me as I walk into the back of his class, but he doesn't take his eyes off his trainees. New Doms, five of them, all hanging on his every word. "This isn't about control. If you're here for that, the exit is right behind you. This is about being a container. About being a safe space for the sub you're with."

He pauses until five heads nod. "The reasons for doing this are different for every Dom. For some, it's about protecting what's soft and courageous and open in the world. For others, it's to be a part of the most beautiful dance there is, the one that happens when a sub makes it to subspace in your hands and takes you somewhere you can't go without him or her."

I've never thought subs were weak, but Quint makes them sound like all the power in the universe rests in their hands.

He scans his five students again. Looking for the unbelievers. "Whatever your reasons are, find them. But no matter why you show up here, once you do, your job is to be a strong container—one that holds steady and doesn't crack and finds just the shape that your sub needs. Those things all take control, but they also take discernment, which is a fancy word for paying fucking attention. It's your job to learn and make smart judgments, because your sub is trusting you, and screwing that up is the worst feeling in the universe."

I swallow, because I know what these five baby Doms don't.

"It will happen." Quint meets my eyes, like he can hear the thoughts in my head. "You will fuck up, because every Dom does, but my job is to make sure it doesn't happen because you're an arrogant jerk who just wants to control another human being."

I don't want to control Ari. I want to be a man strong enough to hold her while she goes somewhere that very few people ever go.

The baby Doms file out past me, a couple casting curious glances, the others looking like the nice, comfortable street they were walking down just exploded. I wait until the last one files out and grin at Quint. "Still terrifying the newbies, I see."

He snorts. "You're still shiny and you're not scared of me at all."

Not much, anyhow, but most baby Doms don't get to screw around in a band with the guy who runs Fettered's training programs. I lean against a wall and try to assemble my words to take a run at what I am scared of. "I'd like to ask for your help."

Quint starts to answer, and then he stops, giving me a much closer perusal. He nods his chin at a couple of the chairs his class just vacated. "Take a seat."

I do. And then I wait quietly for about ten seconds, expecting him to read my mind, before I realize he's not going to drive this conversation, even if he can. I swallow and find my opening beat. "Ari needs a really strong container."

Quint doesn't look surprised—but he doesn't look ready to throw me out the back door, either.

"I'd like you to help me get there. To be the Dom she needs."

He does me the immense favor of not falling off his chair laughing. He just studies me, curious and intense and thoughtful. "What happened to your watch-and-learn shit?"

Fair question, since that's where I was still sitting last night. "She needs me to be faster."

This time I've surprised him. He gives me a long, scary look, the kind that's holding a tape measure to my cock—or maybe my soul. "What is it you think you need to learn?"

Kengali asked loaded questions like that. The answers usually involved six months and a lot of dishwashing. "Where to start. How not to be an asshole."

That gets me a faint twitch of his lips. "Keep it simple. Do what you know how to do. Skills can be learned and she knows that. You need to show her you have some of the rest of the package."

I found some of it in a jam-packed hot yoga studio. "Rhythm."

He raises an eyebrow, but he nods. "Yeah. And patience. Sneak under her skin with that quiet, persistent thing you do."

That's a really big compliment from a guy who rarely hands them out. "She doesn't let trainees do that. Sneak under her skin."

His eyebrow goes up faster this time. I've surprised him again, maybe even impressed him.

I shrug. "I know how to watch."

He nods slowly. "If you do this, you can't do it as a trainee. She has to be able to let go and trust you to get it right, or she'll scene with you a few times and walk away because all you did was scratch a little at her surface."

That would be the part I'm not ready for, but she needs me to step up and try anyhow.

His eyes drill into mine. "If you screw up, every Dom in this place will pound on you."

I can't let that matter. "I will screw up and you're all going to need to deal."

His lips quirk and the Dom stare dials back down to standard hard-ass. "You're not entirely clueless."

That isn't close to good enough—and I'm looking at the one guy who I know will tell me the truth. "Am I crazy to think that I can do this?"

He's silent a long time. "I don't know. But you have two big things in your favor. You're not an arrogant jerk, and you see her strength. You're here because you see that you need to get bigger, instead of thinking about how to make her smaller."

That pisses me off. "Anyone who wants to make Ari smaller is an asshole."

He nods, and the Dom vibe he's been trying to strangle me with eases a little more. "If you remember that, you might have a chance."

It's not a blessing, exactly, but that's okay. He's not the one I need it from.

Chapter Nine

ARI

I wince as Mack lands another technically adequate paddle blow on his wife's ass. Jackie's ready to cry, and for all the wrong reasons.

They waited way too long to come in for help. This is his dream, not hers, and if they don't meet the actual submissive needs written all over her face really soon they're going to lose their chance for kink to add to their marriage instead of damaging it. I watch two more blows, studying Mack's face. Making sure I don't see any of the things that would have me pulling the plug on this entirely.

I don't. He's not an abusive asshole. He's just clueless. He'll learn if he really wants to. A truly great Dom is equal parts inborn and learned, but decent Doms can be trained if they're willing. Mack's only willing on the technical parts right now, and it's my job to fix that. I lean forward and catch the paddle before it lands again, which is a huge breach of etiquette—and one he should have seen coming from ten miles away.

There's no way the steam coming out my ears right now is subtle.

Mack's head jerks up.

I give him the kind of look that tells even a clueless baby Dom it's not his turn to talk. Then I switch my attention to Jackie. "Are you okay lying there for a bit longer, sweetheart, or should we let you up?"

I can see her thinking my question through. Trying to understand what I'm playing at. Jackie's not clueless.

I rub my hand down her arm. Soothing. Asking permission. I need to tell her man some cold, hard truths, and I need her to let me do it. She protects his cluelessness, and if she wants to spend any more time in my world, she needs to stop doing that.

She closes her eyes. Permission granted

I look back at Mack, but he's missed all the nonverbals. One hand absentmindedly strokes his wife's ass, the other studies the paddle.

I solve that by disarming him. "Here's your assignment for the next week."

His eyes fly up to mine again. "Aren't you going to give me some feedback on my paddling skills first?" He looks like a small boy who just dropped his lollipop in the sand. "I've been practicing for weeks."

I give him just enough of what he needs to keep him listening. "Your paddling skills are fine. You've got the angles nicely managed, your blows are consistent in their weight, and your beat was steady." I pause just long enough for him to feel the glow of my words. "Unfortunately, what Jackie needs is entirely different from what you just gave her."

They both jump, him in offense, her in a need to protect that's stymied by all the restraints still holding her. I keep my hand on her arm. In a very real way, I just stepped into this as her temporary Domme.

Mack's lollipop is making him sad again. Which is better than going all arrogant and aggressive, so he gets points for that. "I thought I was doing exactly what Quint taught us to do."

"You did. But Quint was hitting a pillow at the time." I sigh and hope his ears aren't full of sand. "Learning the basics matters, but when you move to a sub instead of a pillow, you need to cue in to what she needs and how she's responding to what you're doing." Also material Quint covered in class.

He nods slowly. "She said she likes it when I practice on her."

She's being hopeful. And overprotective. And trying to fix the scene from the bottom, which is a lot harder to do than when you're the top. "That's a classic newbie sub mistake. She's imagining that one day you're going to wake up after all that practice and realize she's not a pillow."

Jackie's face tightens in shame. I start to lean down, to tell her that her mistake is a small one and easy to make right, when I catch the look on Mack's face.

He's not looking at his paddle anymore. He's looking at his wife, at the emotion written all over her body—and finally realizing that kink is a dance between two people, not between a paddle and an ass.

He moves to squat down beside her, and I shake my head. The last thing she needs right now is for him to get soft and uncertain. I nod my head at his stool and put the paddle back in his hand. "The way she's feeling right now? Chase it away with this."

He looks like I just asked him to beat his wife.

I wait. If they really want this, they need to actually reach out and take it.

The first blow he lands wouldn't squish a fly—but Jackie's breath hitches.

Mack stares at the paddle like it just electrocuted him.

I silently snap my fingers under his nose. He jerks and

applies the paddle to his wife's ass again, this time with enough force to actually dent the fly. Jackie, bless her generous sub heart, makes a cute little noise that clearly runs straight to her husband's ego.

Another blow, and another, his eyes glued to his wife's face. His technique is crap, his aim is worse, and if he doesn't hit her harder soon, Jackie's probably going to scream, but he's found the beginning of the road that might lead to somewhere good.

One baby Dom, back on track. And one trainer who knows just how far he has to go.

Chapter Ten

JACKSON

She's cranky.

I've only caught glimpses of Ari since she emerged from one of the private rooms, but whatever went on back there left her in a piss-poor mood. She's doing a masterful job of not taking it out on anyone else, but that just means it's eating her insides instead.

I look down the bar at where Quint is serving drinks and intermittently fondling his sub's ass. Meghan jumps every time he does it, which even I can figure out means he's torturing her in some inventive way they don't teach to trainee Doms.

I take a big swig of the glass of pink Meghan gave me earlier. I need to stop thinking of myself as a trainee. It might be true, but it's not helpful.

"She was working with a couple from one of our community classes."

I stare at Quint, who somehow snuck over while I wasn't looking. "What?"

"We run a class that introduces light kink for people who have long-term partners and want to add a little spice. One of the couples came in looking for some extra help. She was working with them."

There's no way he's over here to share gossip. "Why did that leave her sad and frustrated?"

His smile is so faint I almost miss it. "She's frustrated because most baby Doms are idiots. She's sad for reasons you'll need to work out for yourself."

I raise an eyebrow. "So you just came over here to refill my drink?"

He snorts. "You're cut off. Any more pink poison and you'll hurt those pretty vocal chords of yours."

Scorpio caught me singing with friends down by the lake last week. She's not listening to my protests that drummers don't sing. "She's trying to turn us into a barbershop quartet."

Quint laughs, loudly enough that half the lounge turns their heads. Including Ari, who gives me a long look that makes her sadder, and then turns away.

Damn.

"Her patience with baby Doms has been going downhill lately." Quint takes away my glass and replaces it with something that looks like plain water.

His tone is friendly, but I hear the warning. Ari isn't just cranky. If I want to have a snowball's chance with her, I need to do it before what's riding her eats any more of her insides. Which means my ass has to get off my stool. Now.

I look deep into my glass of water as my guts congeal into a cool, surreal mass. The last time they did that was a stinking-hot, late-summer day in Gambia. The funeral of Kengali's favorite aunt. He sat down to drum her body home. Ten beats in, he handed me his drum. No words, no looks, no advice. Just the drum.

It was the first time in three years he'd let me touch one.

I look up and let Quint see my resolve. If I could be what

Kengali needed that day, I can damn well be what Ari needs tonight. But I'll take advice if I can get it. "Any suggestions?"

He picks up the cloth he uses to polish his bar. "Keep it simple. BDSM is a head game. You can have a totally effective scene with nothing more than your fingers and your voice."

Interesting advice. "Ari mostly plays with impact toys."

Another faint smile. "I know."

I wait. I know something about this guy's rhythms, and I don't think he's done.

He lifts up my glass and polishes the bottom. "Play the head game with her. See if you can get her to submit to you just a little. Build that trust for her that she can let go with you and you'll catch her."

I meet the gaze of the guy who just promised to be there to catch us both, and then I stand up. I leave my glass. I'm going to be needing my hands.

Chapter Eleven

ARI

I feel him coming before he arrives. I feel him, and I want to turn around and blast him with a temper tantrum of epic proportions, because if he's not a total idiot, and I don't think he is, then he should know I'm riding the edge of hot and unreasonable tonight.

Which isn't his fault, but it means that this is really sucky timing to reach out and touch whatever happened in the yoga studio to see if it has legs.

He stops at my shoulder, and the two subs I'm talking to both go quiet. Which means he's got his Dom face on. I look over, curious, because I'm not sure I've ever actually seen that. And blink.

His entire body is wearing the pure, clean lines of confident Dom. Quiet and understated, but no less potent. I want to scan the lounge, see who's watching, who's noticed, who's putting him up to this. But I'm having a hard time looking away.

He's a match and he's come to play with my fire.

He reaches out a hand toward my elbow and stops. "May I touch?"

This from the guy who gives me easy hugs when I help him lug his drum gear around. He's not asking for permission to put his fingers on my skin—he's asking for permission to change the rules.

On a smarter day, I would say no.

I nod silently. Two can play the game of changing the rules.

He smiles and wraps his fingers around my forearm. No force. Just precision. "Will you come sit with me? I'd like to talk about doing a scene with you tonight."

Lines right out of Negotiation 101. I should know—I wrote them. The first moves to take control of what and where.

My fire decides it wants to play. I let him guide me. Let him feel my resistance, even as I move my feet.

He chuckles in my ear. "I don't scare off that easily, beautiful."

Damn. That's not in the manual. "I'm not trying to scare you. I'm not in the mood to work with a trainee. If that's what you're looking for, I can find someone else to scene with you."

He turns me to face him. "Do I look like a guy who wants a nanny tonight?"

He's not experienced enough to know the misstep he just took. I look up at him with my best brat fluttery eyelashes. "No, Sir."

He busts up laughing, which is totally another misstep, but one that chases some of my pissiness away. Most baby Doms have no idea what to do with a brat, and he doesn't either, but Jackson the drummer thinks I'm funny, and that warms me up a little inside.

I watch, impressed, as he slides back into his Dom skin. He nods his head toward the bar. "Would you like to talk where Quint can listen in?"

I open my mouth to say I'm more than capable of babysitting a negotiation—and then I realize what he's just done. This is a test. Trainees don't have to sit at the bar after they've graduated.

He wants to know if I can let him out of that box in my head.

Tricky baby Dom. I look over at my favorite squishy couch in the corner. "There works."

He guides us there smoothly, like it was his idea. Which is interesting management of the lines of power. He's impressing me so far, even with my crankiest pants on.

He waits until I sit and then takes a seat to my left, turned toward me, his knees locking mine against the couch. Managing the angles. Establishing the physical container. I try to put my checklist away. He's not asking to be a trainee Dom tonight. And my knees feel shivery. I look up at him from under my eyelashes, but this time I'm not bratting. "What did you have in mind, Sir?"

I watch the last word land and run right up his spine. "I'd like to know your hard limits for a scene with someone new."

He didn't ask for the list for someone with his level of experience. I check in with the fire inside me, and I tell him. It's a short list, and a fierce one, and it contains a bunch of kinks he probably can't even spell yet.

He nods like I've just said I prefer milk in my coffee. "Tell me more about why humiliation is a hard limit."

I can feel my eyebrows flying up. Pushy Dom, and he's picked what most would see as the softest kink on my hard limits list for follow-up. "I'd rather save that for a later conversation."

He just holds my eyes.

That's Quint's favorite trick, dammit. I sigh. "Respect really matters to me, and I don't feel respected if my Dom is calling me names or trying to make me feel less than adequate.

I'm not judging the kink, but it absolutely doesn't work for me."

He nods. "What does make you feel respected?"

The fire in me stands up and takes notice. He's not trying to push at my hard stops—he's trying to figure out what makes me tick. That's in the manual, but most Doms take years to notice. I swallow and give him the answer he deserves. "When I'm seen. When my small reactions are noticed. When you call me beautiful and mean it and you're not talking about my body or my face."

He reaches out and strokes his fingers along the tips of my hair, barely touching them. "You're unhappy tonight. Will being seen help with that?"

I blink. "I'm cranky as fuck tonight and you're asking to play with fire."

"No." His voice is quiet, but I hear every word. "I'm asking you to trust me a little bit with what's underneath."

Shit. He clearly doesn't know what singed eyebrows feel like, and somehow, my pissy fire respects that. "I'd like impact play. Something hard enough to get my attention." No way Quint let Jackson graduate without being at least basically competent with a couple of impact toys, but he likely has no idea what I mean by hard. "Partial nudity is fine, penetrative toys and vibes are fine, no sex." I'm being aggressive and I know it, and I know it's because he touched a tender spot.

It's not at all fair to him, but I'm not reasonable Ari tonight.

His knuckles keep playing with the ends of my hair. "Can I touch you with my fingers?"

I blink again. I just offered him pretty much the entire bag of kinky toys. Shiny ones that baby Doms like to think they know how to use. "Yes."

His fingers pause, and then resume their slow foreplay with my hair. "Sexual touch included?"

My knees feel shivery again. "Yes." There's a small voice in the back of my head clearing its throat, because I rarely green-light sexual touch with beginners, but I ignore it. I want him to touch me, and sometimes I need to actually fucking get what I want.

I swallow as I hear the words of my own inner rant. He's going to be my Dom for the next hour or so, and he needs to know how flammable I am tonight. I find my big-girl panties and tug. "I want you to touch me, but I can also feel that I'm pretty unsteady about wanting that."

He smiles, and this time his fingers brush my cheek. "Thank you for telling me."

More lines we teach the beginners, but he means every word. "Any other questions, Sir?"

He shakes his head.

I know all the things he's forgotten. I don't care. Except for one. "I use the club safewords."

He winces, and in that moment, I can see all his uncertainty.

Chapter Twelve

JACKSON

Crap. Beat, totally missed. I can see it all over her face, and I'm sure she can see it all over mine.

I sit up straighter. I meant what I said to Quint yesterday. I'm going to screw up and we're all just going to have to deal. Starting with me. Ari's opened a door that I knocked on with my drums and now I need to walk us through, screw-ups and all. I get my Dom persona back in place and slide my fingers under her chin. It feels huge, touching her like this. Momentous. Important. "I have one ground rule for tonight."

She pauses. Breathes in and out a few times. Settling back into the roles I'm asking us to play. "What is that, Sir?"

I thought it would be entirely weird to be called that, and during our trainee practice sessions, it absolutely was. Now it just feels like an honor. "I want you to stay out of trainer mode. I know you can swim circles around my skills, but I want you to set that down. Safeword out if you need to. Don't rescue us."

There's a moment where I think she's going to refuse, and then her head tilts, resting a little more weight on my hand under her chin. "Why?"

One word, straight into the mess in my guts. "Because I watch you. You don't play for real with baby Doms. You're good, and they learn a lot, but you're not really submitting."

Her eyes flare. I've just stepped on touchy, holy ground. "I submit as much as my Dom can handle."

There's only one way through this, and it's straight in. "That's you making a judgment call, and it's not yours to make tonight. Not if you stay in the scene, anyhow. I know we haven't played together before, and I'm acutely aware that I'm very new. But if we do this, I need you to give that judgment call to me. If I fuck up, safeword out. But until then, the scene is mine and your job is to submit."

I sound like some Dom from a bad kinky movie—but I'm paying attention, and something I've just said has turned a key in a lock somewhere deep inside the woman with her chin in my hand.

She smiles faintly. "Yes, Sir."

She means it. It might have been the most awkward request in the history of kink negotiations, but she got it and she understood and, if I'm reading her signals right, she's glad I made it.

Which means it's time to get off the couch. Except I have no idea where to begin. I have the parameters, and I have a universe of possibilities—and most of them are light years beyond my skills.

I keep touching her hair and holding her chin, because those are the two things keeping this together, and I think. She asked for impact toys, and I know I'm decent with them for a beginner because most of them are just oddly shaped drum sticks. But I'm also looking at my two hands and what they're doing right now. The hands she's permitting to hold her. I don't want to give that up.

I reach down beside me for the bag that rarely leaves my

side and pull out the first drum I ever made. I set it down between my knees and shift my gaze back to Ari. She's not watching me anymore. She's staring at my drum. I put a single finger under her chin and tip her wide eyes up to meet mine. "Dance for me, beautiful."

Chapter Thirteen
ARI

He's surprised me.

I'm so rarely surprised anymore, and my insides are turning over in response to what he's just done. He's supposed to head me for the nearest bench or set of chains and get me firmly under his physical control. That's what we teach. Let the restraints help you. I taught him how to adjust cuffs myself.

He taps his finger under my chin. "Stand up, head down and eyes closed, hands behind your back."

Part of me hears his green as he realizes that I need more instructions if he's going to keep control of the shape of this scene. Part of me shivers. He's choosing to restrain me with nothing more than his voice and my obedience.

That's a ballsy move. Which is either an accident or he's been watching me well enough to know just how much I like it when a Dom makes me fight with myself. I stand slowly and follow his directions. The shivers in my belly have earned him this much.

I feel him move past me, and I hear the slide of furniture and the soft, calm murmur of his voice as he gives instructions to someone else. I'm not surprised people are helping. Scening in the lounge technically isn't allowed without permission, but everyone will assume he has mine. Not to mention the other Doms in the band who've been breaking that rule for months.

I know why he's doing it. This is his turf. He's comfortable in here. He knows how to work the space, the audience, the props.

My belly shivers again. Fettered is my turf, and very few people who play with me are smart enough to rebalance that. I still don't know if Jackson is pulling this off through dumb luck or something else, but his first couple of steps have unsettled me in ways no one has managed for a long time.

His breath slides warm against my ear. "You're going to dance for me now. I've cleared space behind you. I'm going to go sit with my drum, and when you hear my beat begin, I want you to open your eyes. They're to stay on me. You can watch my face, my hands, my shoelaces—it doesn't matter, so long as your eyes are on me."

My brat makes a solemn vow to do nothing but stare at his balls. "Yes, Sir."

His hands stroke the bare skin of my arms, down to where my wrists are joined behind my back. He gently moves my hands apart. The shaking in my belly levels up.

I wait, expecting an order to undress. Getting a sub naked is standard Dom operating procedure.

His hands move, gliding up the soft blue velvet of the mini skirt and corset Chloe made for me. I've barely taken them off since I unwrapped them. "I like who you are when you wear this. Keep it on."

My head reels. He's breaking every damn rule there is—and keeping the most important one. He has my utter and complete attention.

Another breath down the back of my neck and he's gone. Not far. I feel him settling into the couch at my knees. The soft sounds of leather squishing. The barest of air currents moving by my legs. His fingers touch the inside of one of my knees and skim upward, a slow, attention-getting feather. They pause at the hem of my mini skirt, which I now know is about four inches too long.

I hear my soft whimper and the way he breathes it in.

His fingers trace light circles on the soft swell of my inner thigh.

I want to melt right where I stand.

Chapter Fourteen

JACKSON

I don't want to move. Ever. I could sit right here like this, in the glow of Ari's dawning arousal and my aching need, and never leave.

But neither of us are ready for that.

I slide my fingers away more slowly than I've ever done anything in my life, put both hands on the well-worn leather of my drum, and start tapping a slow beat.

My head is already wincing—it was ages ago I gave her my instructions, and I should have repeated them. My hands don't panic. They know there's a language that doesn't need any words. I call to the blood that lives in her veins, to the legacy of ancestors who were born dancing and died that way. *Move. Feel my beat. Let my drum move you.*

Her body starts a slow sway, one that jitters a bit as her head tries to intervene.

I let my hands keep talking. *Dance for me, beautiful.*

Slowly, the beat moves up from her feet into hips encased in blue velvet. I don't push. I want her to stay there for a while, to find all the range in the part of her body where the people of Gambia believe the soul lives. Fertile, sacred, sexy hips.

I can see people forming a semi-circle behind her. I wrap them in with my hands. I used to play for a single dancer in front of the fire all the time. The performer and the drum are everything. Anyone else is just shadows—but shadows matter. Shadows bask in the rays of the dancer and all of who she becomes.

I hide a grin. Ari's eyes are still closed, and she's still dancing like an urban white kid, all contained and neat. I put a more primal energy into my hands. A sensual one. Teasing her with the touch of my drums.

Her arms jerk away from her body and then right back down. Her eyes open, grabbing for mine like a lifeline—and then like someone she wants to stab.

Shit. Nobody in Africa gets mad when you drum them a dance. My hands move to soothe, but that's the wrong answer. I'm not here as her drummer. I'm here because I asked to be her Dom. Which means she doesn't get to stand there and glare at me.

I don't bother adding that to my mental list of screw-ups. At this point I just have to live with the fact that they're going to be legion. Instead, I meet her eyes with the steadiest look I can manage and add demand into my hands. *Dance, beautiful. NOW.*

There's a moment when I'm not sure I've won, but then she capitulates. Sort of. Her temper moves into her hips and locks them up, making her movements jerky. Tense. Awkward. A dancer headed straight for the kind of humiliation that is one of her hard limits.

I've somehow managed to dump totally exhibitionist Ari into the one thing she doesn't want to do for an audience.

I gulp, because my nice simple scene just crashed into hard and I can see the problem but I have no idea how to fix it. Enough time and enough drumming and a little light teasing and I could get her through this, but those aren't the right tools for tonight. I wanted to have control and I need to use it. I thought we could recreate some of the magic that happened in the yoga studio and use that as our foundation, but I'm staring straight at a crack that's about to break this thing all to hell.

There's probably a list of ways a mile long to fix it, but I can only think of one. I need to collect my sub back up and head into territory she knows better than the lands where I just tried to take her. I lift my drum, keeping up a one-handed beat, and head over to Eli's cello set-up, hastily borrowed for my scene. Barstool seat for me with a box to elevate my drum and my feet. I assemble myself without rushing—that much of Quint's training has stuck. Then I beckon Ari forward.

She steps toward me, her forehead wrinkling in confusion, her hips still doing their awkward, cranky dance.

I put my hand on her hip as she arrives, bringing her to my side. Physically using my drum and my hand to gently pulse her hips. Letting her feel one simple, steady message.

It might be a really small container and a really small dance —but I've got her.

He's trying to fix it. I swallow the bitter taste rising up my throat. He couldn't have known. I'm not sure anyone at the club knows that no matter how big a show-off I am in everything else, I only dance in crowds. Leftover trauma from a ballet teacher who wanted my body, but not my soul.

In ten years of kink, it's never come up—and poor Jackson somehow stepped into that quagmire in the first three steps of a virgin scene.

I breathe again and feel him breathing with me. Feel his solid, steady grip, gently swaying my hips. His thumb strokes the inch of bare skin between my corset and skirt, asking a little more of me to move. Giving me something to move with.

A dance my body understands.

I huff out a soft sigh as the tight threads inside me begin to loosen back up, and belatedly remember I'm supposed to be looking at him. I open my eyes and let him see my gratitude. *Nice save, sexy drummer man.*

He smiles a little and his hand slides down, briefly cupping me in a way that has my brat gasping for air, and then continuing his journey until his fingers are skimming the swell of my inner thigh where he began. His drum quiets a little. "Touch yourself, Ari."

I blink. I can usually read where a scene is going in my sleep. This one has taken a wrecking ball to my sub psychic powers.

He grins, and it's full of pleased cockiness. "We're going to try a different kind of dancing. Show me how your fingers and your pussy like to move together."

That's a standard Dom trick, but he's not going to be able to see much with my clothes still on. I slide my thumb under the waistband of my mini skirt and wait. Maybe he'll get the message.

His fingers tap away on the drum, unconcerned.

Fine. Whatever. Not rescuing. I shove my hand down inside the skirt, which is a tight fit, and an interesting kind of bondage. I aim something fairly close to a glare in his direction.

He's not ruffled at all. "Eyes on me. Let your fingers move to the beat of my drum."

Pushy Dom. I slide my fingers into the folds of my pussy, annoyed at how wet I am. This is the most uncomfortable scene I've been in for a long time, and it shouldn't be arousing.

I play with my wetness a little, trying to get my head back in the right game. He didn't want a trainer, but he doesn't deserve this, either. He's made a simple request. Touch myself. Give over some of my arousal to his drums. Let him see.

Let him see.

The twisted wires in my head finally straighten out and I do what I should have done right from the beginning. I stop moving. This is just like hot yoga. Let him see that I don't know where to go yet. Let him and his beat come find me.

A long, slow breath and the tide rises inside me, easy and

cheerful and free. Welcoming the simple pleasure of slick fingers and slick folds and a body that always enjoys a quickie, even if it's one by my own hands.

Jackson's drum speeds up, encouraging my fingers as I find my most responsive places. This won't take long. I'm craving release now, and enjoying the man who's helping me get there. I look at him and let him see the pathway I've found. We've got this.

The drum thunks hard and shifts gears.

I stare at the guy who just crashed my nicely building orgasm into a wall. *On purpose.*

He picks up the beat again, but it's different this time. Asking for something different.

I grit my teeth as I hear what it's telling me. He's not asking. His drum is speaking with freaking Dom voice. He wants the orgasm he *takes*, not the one I give.

Which is total justice for the shit I just pulled. I was topping from the bottom without even thinking about it, and his fingers, calmly tapping on that damn circle of leather, are letting me know that he's happy to crash me into a wall any time I might like to try that particular form of disrespect again.

I swallow, and my throat is dry. He might not have chosen an impact toy for my ass, but he's somehow found a really good one for my brain.

I meet his eyes and nod. Message received.

I get a faint smile, and an even fainter nod of approval.

My brat tries to rise again, and I totally know why. He has me squirming, and it's not because he wants me to come on command. It's the way he's asking me to come. His drum is speaking of breaths by my ear and feather touches on the insides of my thighs.

He doesn't want my fast, fiery quickie. He wants me to open first.

I swallow, but the desert in my throat hasn't changed. This is dancing all alone with everybody watching, only worse, and I have no idea how he's finding all my fragile places in one scene, but he is.

His eyes are glued to mine. Two dark, steady, seeing rocks.

My body is responding, because this is exactly what it wants. Surrender into the hands of a man strong enough to catch me. But my body is an idiot, because we've careened off brick walls this entire scene, and not all of them are his, and whatever promises his hands might be whispering in the dark of my lounge, he's not ready for me to be that open. That soft. To be all in with all my fragile places and my hard ones.

The wetness under my fingers changes to the distinctive glide that comes right before a really good orgasm. I curse silently. I don't want to give him a soft orgasm, but he's pulling one out of me anyhow.

The beat of his drum thrums straight into in my pussy. Asking me to let myself head over that swell.

I don't know why I'm resisting. I orgasm as easily as I breathe, but this one doesn't feel easy. I'm back to awkward, and I don't like it. We've landed ourselves in a scene with too much demand and not enough trust, and only one of us knows that, and I need to do something or we're going to break.

I don't want us to break. Jackson doesn't deserve to have me safeword out. He's earned that much of my respect. I might not be as excited to play with baby Doms as I once was, but I don't humiliate them.

I gather myself. A small orgasm doesn't need me to let go much, and I'm really close. I can give him that and we can all go home mostly unbroken.

A firm hand cups me over my fingers and the drum stops dead.

I open my eyes, and Jackson's are right there in front of my nose.

Wide open, glued to mine, and mad as hell.

Chapter Sixteen

JACKSON

I have no idea what just happened, but she wrapped something up and took it away, and that's not okay. She's not faking her pleasure—not exactly. But she's not all here anymore either, and somehow I can tell.

My brain spins, trying to figure out what just went wrong. Quint's training lessons race through my head. Sometimes scenes take a hard turn. There are two choices when that happens—double down or change it up. That sounded obvious when I was sitting in a chair with a notepad in front of me. Right now, with Ari three seconds from orgasm and running away as fast as she can, I have no idea what to do.

So I stick with where I am. My hand over hers. My eyes, reaching out and trying to call her back. "I want real, Ari. It doesn't have to be big, but I want real." I gulp and add the words I hope like hell she needs. "Or we're done here."

She stares at me, our eyes conjoined in frozen, fragile intimacy. And then slowly, so slowly that I don't feel it at first, she starts to move. Not her hands. The rest of her, shimmying ever so slightly to a beat that doesn't exist anymore except in her head.

I slide the hand that isn't cupping her back over to my drum. With that same aching slowness that's coming from somewhere deep inside her, I pick up a beat and put it in both my hands. One that only she and I will feel. I keep my eyes on hers. *Stay with me, beautiful. Be real.*

Her eyes glisten, and she whimpers, low and quiet and gorgeous.

I add a little weight to my cupped fingers, drumming on the backs of hers. Sending tremors into the core of who she is.

She moves her fingers under mine, ever so slightly. Not taking charge this time. Asking.

I could let her. Some really important part of her has just let go for me, and I could make this easy and let her finish this with the fast, raucous orgasm she clearly wants. But right here, in this moment, I've just learned something huge about myself.

I don't want the one that's easy for her to give.

I want the one that's hard. The one that's soft and gentle and open and lets me look, for just a heartbeat or two, at the most vulnerable parts of who she is.

I ease the beat of both my hands, whispering a message to drum and pussy both. No pushing, no demand at all. Just invitation and a promise. *I'm here.*

The breath that whispers out of her is so quiet I don't even hear it—I just feel it on my cheek. And then she lets go, a gentle rain on my fingers as her head drifts down to my shoulder.

I sit there, as stunned as I've ever been in my life. There might only be two people in this lounge who know she's just come, but she has, and my shoulder and my hand are all that are left holding her up.

I scoop her into my arms, dizzy on the high of what she's just given me—and crash into the awkward realities of trying to sit two people on a bar stool when one of them doesn't have any bones left and the other one has a drum between his legs that's trying to dump him on his ass.

Eli and Quint swoop in with a huge armchair an instant later, clearly veterans of saving idiot Doms from themselves. I manage to stay on my feet long enough to settle into the expanse of leather with Ari on my lap, holding her like the delicate spun glass she is, gasping for air like I just ran a marathon and don't care if everyone knows it.

I run my hand down her hair and pull her in tighter. I don't know what she needs for aftercare, but I need this. I need to hold my gift and savor every precious bit of it.

She curls into my chest. An answer with no words.

Quint delivers two water bottles to a side table within easy reach, approval in his eyes.

I sit, and hold, and breathe, and wait.

My marathon isn't over yet. It's not his approval that matters.

Chapter Seventeen

ARI

Holy fucking hell.

I've spent more time in aftercare than most people do in a lifetime. I know what it is to have wobbly legs and an even more wobbly brain, and a big part of me lives to go through the experiences that make me feel like that.

But this isn't one of them. Not yet, and it's not because of him.

I screwed up and I'm not even entirely sure why, but both of us deserve for me to figure it out. I raise my head, which is way harder than it should be, and manage to find his eyes. "I'm so sorry, Jackson. I fucked up. Thank you for not dropping me."

His eyebrows fly up. "Hard on yourself much?"

Not usually. I frown. I know, better than anyone, that wobbly brains need time to steady before they assemble reasonable thoughts—but I also know that gold lives in the wobbles.

His hand strokes my hair, cuddling my head back into his chest. Giving me the touch we both obviously need. "Tell me what that was like for you."

I don't know where to start, but I have enough experience to know that pretty much anywhere will eventually work. "I don't like dancing where other people can see me. Where they're focused on me."

I feel his wince. "Yeah, I figured that out. I'm sorry."

He shouldn't be. "I didn't tell you. It's not even something I've thought of for a long time. You see me dance in the crowd while the band is playing all the time. It was a perfectly reasonable assumption." I sigh and cuddle in a little tighter. "And you're a Dom. You're under no obligation to keep me comfortable."

"Granted." His hand rubs small circles on my lower back. "But I didn't clear that general kind of activity with you first, and I should have. I'm pretty sure you taught that class."

Brave baby Dom. "You did fine, Jackson. This is on me." I can feel his disagreement rippling against my cheek and know I need to fix it. "You had my complete attention. Even when you told me I was going to dance for you. I didn't expect you to be able to set a scene that well, and you totally had me."

His chuckle is mostly rueful. "Glad to know I got the first ten seconds right."

This conversation isn't going how it needs to go. I sit up and let him see my resilience along with my wobbles. "Pretend you're not a baby Dom for a minute and I'm not the most experienced person you've ever touched. Tell me the story of what you think happened in that scene, the same way you'll tell it to Quint when he asks."

He takes a breath and nods. "Okay. I thought it started well. The negotiations felt strange, but good. It felt like you trusted me with some pieces of you, and other than forgetting to ask for your safewords, I wasn't a total moron."

I smile a little and say nothing. It's his story we're chasing right now, not mine. I'm chasing it for murky reasons, but I can at least get the listening part right.

His eyes narrow. "You were okay when I pulled out my drum. Things didn't go sour until I had you back away from the couch." Comprehension dawns, and with it, self-recrimination. "Until I stopped touching you. That was a mistake. I saw how well you responded to touch when we were negotiating. I let you anchor to that and then I took it away."

I snort. "Do you want your sub comfortable at the beginning of a scene, Sir?" I let fully sardonic Ari infuse that last word.

He rolls his eyes and shifts me so that I'm straddling his lap. "No, especially when she's a brat. But I don't want her feeling abandoned, either."

I shake my head. "I'm still not sure what was going on for me, but that wasn't it. Or not most of it, anyhow. You had me. Verbal restraints, eyes on you, picking up on the threads of what started in the yoga studio yesterday—you had me attentive and interested and unsteady. Then I ran into something."

He nods slowly. "Yeah. I saw it happen. I just didn't fucking know what to do about it."

I look, but he's not beating himself up for it anymore. Which is interesting and damn attractive. I'm good at soothing Dom egos and newbie nerves, but he doesn't need me to. Which is a really good thing because my wobbles need him on his feet—and he's found them. I nod wordlessly. I'm still telling too much of this story.

He runs his palms up my thighs. Grounding me, very literally. "I tried going back to basics. Touch. Anchoring. Somewhere more steady for you." His cheeks turn a little red. "I maybe leaned on your experience too hard, but I figured you would be comfortable touching yourself while people watched."

I snort again. "Duh."

He grins and a little more of the stress between us transmutes into something different. He shrugs, looking tentative for the first time since I got my bones back. "I thought what happened after that was amazing. You let me get the scene back on track. And then you let me hold you while you let go."

I give him a dirty look. "That is so not what happened and you know it. Own what the fuck you did there, Sir."

He blinks, even as his spine firms. "I'm not wrong about the first part. You helped me fix what was wobbling."

I nod. "A little. Maybe. I'm not sure you needed my help. That drum of yours is a pushy bitch."

He laughs. "She'll be pleased you think so." He takes a breath. "She would have let you have your fast orgasm. It was me who didn't. I wanted more from you, and I still feel about a hundred feet tall that you gave it to me."

Those are the words I was waiting for. The ones that acknowledge that he took and demanded that I give. "Pushy Dom."

His chest doesn't puff up, but the rest of him is practically incandescent. "Yes. Thank you for trusting me that much."

My eyes burn. I'm not sure I do.

Chapter Eighteen

JACKSON

I've stepped wrong again. Not a lot wrong, but with Ari, nuance matters. I rub my thumb along her cheekbone, taking in the sheen of wet in her eyes that wasn't there before. "Talk to me, beautiful."

She sighs. "I'm worried that I let go like that because I really need to. That I might have been too quick to trust." She swallows. "Which will end up hurting both of us."

Whoosh. Time for me to stop being a baby Dom worried he screwed up his first real scene. Past time. "That's bullshit."

Her eyes widen.

I keep blundering ahead, even though I feel like a giant in a dollhouse. "You're honestly going to go with the story that maybe you went too easy on me and gave me something I hadn't earned yet just because I asked really nicely?"

Her smile is slow, and self-deprecating, and maybe even appreciative. "Okay, maybe not." She sighs and swipes a hand under her nose. "I was a hard-ass sub, and I'm sorry for that."

"I'm not." My fingers grip her chin, because some of how I felt when she melted on my hand has finally found its way to my spine. "I don't want you to go easy on me. I want you to be real."

She nods slowly. "You said that during the scene too. It really matters to you."

"Real is everything." I lean forward and kiss her nose. "Now tell me about the real that you ran into that made you want to ditch a nice orgasm and get the hell out."

She blinks at me for a really long time. I let her stew in it. I might not be good at much of this Dom gig yet, but I know how to watch and I want her to know it.

She glares at me. "I'm not sure."

I snort. "Not good enough. You're the most self-aware kinky person I know. Figure it out."

Her glare morphs almost instantly into a rueful grin. "Shit, you pull that Dom stuff out of your pocket really fast sometimes."

I'll make an offering at the altar of Quint's training classes as soon as we're done. "You're avoiding my question."

She rolls her eyes, and I'm pretty sure I should do something about that, but I'm not going to. She takes in another deep breath and lets it out—and when she does, her face changes. There's embarrassment there. And guilt. And something darker. Shame, maybe. "I was telling myself that you didn't deserve for me to safeword out, and I could offer up a baby orgasm and somehow make it all okay." Her voice gets really quiet. "By faking and lying to my Dom."

Real. A mountain of it, right here in my lap. I cup her face in my hands, wanting her to see just how huge that is for me. "I felt you trying to take some of who you are out of the scene."

Her eyelids slink shut, and there are tears behind them. "I know, and I'm so sorry. That's not who I am. That's not how I play, ever."

I lean in and drop kisses on her wet lashes. "It was how you played today. Thank you."

Her eyes fly open. "What?"

I let my thumb catch the single tear that falls. Not wiping it away. Just holding it. "It means that some part of what we did together stretched you. You let me take you that deep."

She sighs. "And then I tried to run."

I grin. "You came back."

She makes a face. "Pushy Dom."

My turn to tell the truth. "Yup. Maybe not from the right place, though. I was pretty angry that you tried to leave."

She nods slowly. "Yes, you were. I deserved every bit of it, though. And honestly, it probably took seeing that for me to trust you with what you were asking for." She bites her bottom lip, but her eyes never waver from mine. "That's one of my secrets, Jackson. I trust a little very easily. But I find it hard to trust a lot, and I need to trust a lot to let go and be soft like you were asking me to do."

I let myself hear all the layers of her words, even though some of them are hard. She's not sure she should have trusted me that much. She has doubts, maybe even regrets. And she's showing me at least the outline of one of her secrets.

I nestle my cheek into hers.

As beginnings go, I can live with that. I haven't earned her, not nearly. But I've earned myself a chance. She tried to slam the door shut and I didn't let that happen, and now I get to see what I can make of it.

No pressure.

Chapter Nineteen

ARI

I walk into Quint's office. I know he'll be waiting, and it's for the same reason that I'm walking through his door. Someone needs to rake me over the coals.

He closes the single file folder on his desk and raises his eyebrow. "Where's Jackson?"

"Walking home with Harlan and Scorpio." Who bribed him with a potent combination of sushi and threats and friendship. They'll make sure he lands gently off his Dom high.

"Good." Quint puts his feet on his desk.

I sit down in a chair on the other side and do the same, wiggling my bare toes. "I fucked up, Quint—and I almost dumped a baby Dom on his ass in his first big scene."

"Does he know how big it was?"

I shake my head. "No. He knows it wasn't small, and he sees most of what he did pretty clearly, but he doesn't have enough context to know just how close we came to disaster."

A long, slow look, and one I thoroughly deserve. "Does he know you contemplated safewording out?"

I nod. "I told him. But he felt what happened. He knew I was trying to hide from him."

I don't miss the glint of trainer pride in Quint's eyes. "Good."

Coals don't always have to look hot to feel that way.

"So." Quint swings his feet down and wraps his hands around my bare toes. "You're not here to whine that he wasn't strong enough to hold you, which is how both of us figured this might go down."

I wince. "Yeah. He did good. Really great, actually." Quint knows the list of where Jackson screwed up as well as I do, but he also knows none of it mattered. I know exactly how melty I got when my Dom ran his fingers up the inside of my thighs. Everything that went wrong after that is on me. "He's got good instincts for the head game."

"He's observant and he's in this for all the right reasons, and we're not here to talk about Jackson."

I glare, because this Dom won't let me get away with shit, even when he's mostly being my friend. "It's part of why I'm here."

"The last part." He hands me a bottle of water. "If you want someone to hold your hand and let you cry first, go find Mattie or Meghan or Sam."

"Asshole."

He snorts. "Drink. That scene was big for you too."

Bigger for me than it was for a baby Dom, and there's all kinds of wrong in that. I take a deep breath. No, not wrong. Scary. And maybe something that could be the beginnings of right if I can get my head screwed on straight and my ass out of whatever teakettle I just stuck it in. "The easy story is that he pushed, with reasonably good aim, and there wasn't enough trust between us yet for me to hand over my submission."

Quint raises an eyebrow. "He's really gotten to you."

I eye him, deeply suspicious of his tone. "Why do you say that?"

He smirks. "Because he barely had to look at you before you came. And because you never hand out this much bullshit."

Asshole. "I mostly stayed out of the bullshit with him in aftercare."

A skeptical look. "He's too green to know where he should have kept pushing. I'll talk with him."

That's exactly what I don't need—a baby Dom with good instincts and a really obnoxious coach. "This is for him and me to figure out."

"Right. That's why you're in my office."

Dammit. "I'm here because I was a total brat tonight and I tried to fuck over a newbie and somebody needs to help me figure out why."

Quint's chuckles bust out of him before I finish speaking.

I glare at him some more. "What?"

He stops, and leans forward, and his eyes are full of the compassion he rarely lets anybody see. "I'm happy for you, Ari. Really happy."

I blink. "What?"

He tucks my hair behind my ear. "When seasoned veterans start fucking up basic scenes and dishing out crap after, it means something. Welcome to being kinky and human and annoyed as fuck at the latter."

I stare at him.

His hands are gentle, but his eyes aren't letting me move anywhere. "It means your heart got involved, sweetheart."

It bothers me that my first reaction is to punch him in the nose. "Shut up. We're nowhere near that. He's just a guy. An interesting one, but that's all. I was just having a fragile day when he showed up."

He grins and leans back. "I fucked up every scene I did with Meghan. For months."

I wince, partly at his theory, and partly because I remember.

Quint's face is in hard-ass-friend mode, but his eyes are still gentle. "You've been sitting there waiting for the right guy to show up for you. Now maybe he has, and you tested him tonight, and he stood up."

Rocks land on my most tender places. "He did. I didn't."

"That's what you need. Someone who can hold his shit together even when you don't."

The acid burns all the way up from the depths of my belly. "And you think I should trust a baby Dom to be that for me?"

"Hell, no. Trust has to be earned, especially with how hard you want to throw yourself against it." He watches me, and I know I'm standing right at the edge of the coals. "But you need to consider giving the guy who melted you into putty tonight a chance to show you what else he's got."

Chapter Twenty
JACKSON

I have a plan.

I didn't when I fell into bed last night, high and exhausted and with most of my brains still splattered all over the floor of Fettered's lounge, but this morning I woke up knowing I needed one. Kengali taught me that. Good music is a whole lot more than the first few beats, especially if you're playing with someone else.

I walked into this thinking that Ari and everyone else was going to have to give me time and space to screw up and klutz around and find my feet. Last night she put me on notice— she's going to need that kind of space too. Which is both beautiful and wholly terrifying, and means my plan needs a container that's a whole lot bigger than a bar stool in a lounge with several dozen of our friends watching.

Fortunately, six years in Africa taught me a whole lot about space and time. It looked lazy to me at first, but I got over that about the same time I realized that I hadn't been lonely for months.

Somewhere deep inside Ari, I think she's lonely.

I pick up my phone, because walking over to her hut isn't quite as easy here as it was in Gambia. I've already sent her several texts. This is just me hovering until she decides to show up. Or not, but I'm pretty sure Ari doesn't back away from much, and I'm not all that scary to her yet, no matter what happened last night.

It takes me a minute to realize the knocking isn't coming from my phone. Which maybe suggests I don't have as many of my brains gathered back up as I was thinking, but that's okay. I open my door and pull her in fast, because my wimpy heating system took a while to get my apartment to this temperature and a late-fall Seattle day could take that apart fast.

She gapes, first at me, and then at the set-up she can see in my living room.

I grin. "Come on in. The heat's intentional. Clothing is up to you."

She collects herself fast, which doesn't surprise me at all, and reaches out a finger, lightly tracing through the hair on my chest and tugging on the waistband of the light pants I'm wearing. "I'm good with fewer clothes."

I laugh and back away, because Ari on the prowl is going to be a lot of fun one day, but I have something slightly different in mind for this afternoon. "I have hot drinks or cold ones. Preference?"

She takes a curious sniff. "What country did I just walk into?"

"Gambia." I pick up a jug of iced wonjo juice and pour. "I went there right after university to try to do good deeds, and fell in. Stayed six years, learned to play the drums."

Her head tips to the side a little. "Part of you is still there."

I'm not the only one who watches. "Yeah. I've been back here three years, but it's still hard."

She's wearing her quizzical bird face. "Why kink?"

I could give her an answer, and I will, but this plan has more parts than just getting her in my door. I reach out and take her hand, juggling two glasses in the other as I lead her over to the mountain of pillows in the middle of my living room. "I'm not sure whether to call this a scene or not, but I have some ideas for today, and I'd like you to let me take charge of the shape of our afternoon."

Her eyes run over the carefully laid-out plates and pillows and cozy blankets. "This looks like a really high-class, funky slumber party."

There won't be any sleeping. Not if I'm doing my job anything close to right. I point her at the pile of pillows closest to the small electric fireplace that's the main reason I took this place. Bowls of water are steaming on the top. I mostly use them to maintain humidity for my drums, but today I'm hoping they create the right environment for something quite different.

Ari sinks to her knees and turns slowly in a circle, reaching out to touch fabrics. "These are beautiful."

I laugh quietly. "I'll show you the really ugly ones I made later. These were done by some of the more talented villagers where I lived. Farewell gifts, mostly." They understood what I was coming home to, even if I didn't, and they sent what company they could.

She traces a line of delicate, difficult embroidery. "They love you."

What of me they could understand. "Yes. Very much." I take a seat behind her and tip her over gently onto a convenient pile of pillows.

She looks up at me, eyes open and wide and curious.

Part of me wants nothing more than to spoon her for hours in front of the fire, but we need to get somewhere more solid first. Last night's most subtle lesson drummed its way into me sometime in the deep dark of night while I was sleeping.

Ari doesn't trust easy. She needs hard to feel safe.

Chapter Twenty-One

ARI

This is moving quickly. I look up at the excellent view of Jackson's chest, glistening in the heat, and take a moment to appreciate wherever he's taking us.

He looks down at me. "Are you going to stay in all of those clothes?"

He shouldn't be giving me a choice, but I'm not dumb enough to stay in a wool sweater in the savannah. I sit up and strip down to a cami and knickers.

He runs his fingers under the strap of the cami and pushes me back into a gentle recline on the pillows. His other hand reaches for one of the morsels on the plate next to my knee and offers it to me.

I wait to see if he's going to tell me what it is.

His lips quirk. "No food allergies. I checked."

He read my member form and he doesn't plan to kill me. Good. I eye the bite in his fingers suspiciously. I don't know anything about Gambian food, but I have an Ethiopian friend who thinks nothing is spicy enough unless it makes you cry.

Jackson chuckles and keeps holding the darn food at my lips.

I open as gracefully as I can given that I've just contem-plated mutiny.

He smiles and drops the morsel on my tongue.

I groan, because whatever he dipped it in is sweet with a little kick and tastes of lands I need to visit yesterday. "You have a whole plate of those, right?"

He laughs. "Yes, actually. With several sauces. But since they're one of my favorites too, you'll have to earn them."

That's never a good line to hear from your Dom. I give him the hairy eyeball he deserves. "What do you mean, Sir?"

He reaches over and picks up a velvet bag, upending it just outside the nest of pillows.

My eyes quickly roam the contents. Feather tickler, lube, anal plug, nipple clamps, an assortment of small vibrators, and what looks like a couple of the small impact toys we issue to people who shouldn't be swinging anything bigger.

He cups my breast and kneads gently. "Anything in there a hard limit?"

Not since about a month after I got kinky. "No."

He rolls my nipple between two fingers. "Anything in there you're taking seriously?"

I make a face. "No. Sorry."

He just grins at me. "Good."

That's a frightening answer. I wonder if he knows it.

He scoops up the toys and puts them in a bowl. "Fingers. Full access."

Cripes, we're already negotiating in shorthand. "No breath play. Otherwise, fine."

His eyes bulge.

Too bad. I play in the big leagues where stuff like that needs to be said.

He swallows it back down. "Got it. Thank you. Okay,

ground rules. We're going to have a conversation. Twenty questions. I get to ask one, then you do."

Smart man. If I go first, he's going to be so shocked he forgets his nice list of starter questions. However, this is one of my favorite games, so I won't argue. "Sounds like fun."

He frowns a little. "This next part might be a little messy to define, but I want your words to be free of the scene. You can answer however you want, and ask whatever you want, but your body is mine. No touching or major moving unless I tell you to."

Not as messy as he thinks. And once again, he's managed to get my full attention. "Understood."

"Your safewords are the same as last night? Red and yellow?"

I nod. "Always." I just can't wrap my head around yelling "zucchini" or "toaster" if the world needs to end.

He starts to say something, and then pauses. "If we fall asleep later, is that okay for you?"

I look around at the pillows and the fire and the food. I know why he's asking, because I ran headlong into a brick wall he wasn't expecting last night and he doesn't want to leave me weirdly vulnerable, but he's built us a nest and I can totally see napping with him here. "That sounds heavenly, actually."

He grins and pops another bite of bliss in my mouth, this time dipped in a new flavor. "Good. Then it's time for my first question."

I wait. There's no way he can come up with anything I haven't been asked a million times before.

He takes a minute, watching my face as he thinks.

I'm surprised. I figured he would have his questions lined up, waiting to pounce when he thinks I least expect them.

His hand moves to cup my breast again, finding the exact

kneading pressure to drive me slowly crazy. "If you were going to sing right now, what would your song be?"

I stare at him. "I'm not singing. Hard limit."

He laughs. "I've heard you sing and you're not as bad as you think. But this is just about the musical selection. No singing required."

His fingers slide under the hem of my cami and the feel of his drumming calluses on my warm skin chases whatever I was going to say right out of my head.

He chuckles, and his fingers roll my nipple. "Pick a song, Ari. Which one captures how you feel right now?"

I know the answer, and it makes me squirm. Which straightens my spine and pushes my breast up into his hand, because I might be a lot of things I don't expect with him, but I'm not someone who hides. "That new one of Quint's. The ballad. The one that has you believing it's all soft and warm and then it surprises you with gravelly bits and that low part he does in the middle."

The light in Jackson's eyes is amused and pleased. "We tease him about that being his cranky-lover song."

That so totally nails everything about Quint and his song that I have to laugh. And groan, because this man really knows what he's doing with a nipple.

He gives it one more roll and slides his hand away, down to my waist. "Your turn to ask a question, beautiful."

Chapter Twenty-Two

JACKSON

I expect her first question to be lethal. Scorpio clued me in on the walk home last night that this is one of Ari's favorite games.

She almost speaks, and then she pauses, frowning.

I pick up a tassel, a poor, misshapen thing made of grass back when I was first trying to make friends with Gambia. It's a bit prickly, just like the woman lying on my pillows in her underwear. I trace it up her inner thigh.

She sighs. "Somehow, you know how to call out both my softness and my desire to be a totally immature brat."

I'm pretty sure those two things are connected—and maybe even a good sign. "Ask whatever you want, Ari. Words aren't going to break me."

She looks at me, almost bashful. "I know that."

She needs to know it down where her brat lives, because that's the doorway to what she protects most. I run the tassel up onto her belly, tracing sworls on the silk of her cami.

She shivers and laughs. "Okay, a question I already asked and you didn't answer. Why kink?"

Not lethal. I let the tassel run up over a covered breast and grin as her nipple puckers under the silk. "Drummers are a bit like Doms. We hold containers for people to let out all of who they are." A catharsis that happened every day in a dusty village in Gambia. "People don't usually dance like that here, so when I got back, I suddenly had this hole inside myself. About nine months ago a friend took me to a play party."

She's looking straight at me, really listening. "Smart friend."

I shrug. "It was a bit of a hot mess, actually, but I saw something I hadn't seen for a couple of years. And I met Eli there, which led to some interesting chats about music and other things. Eventually that turned into a spot in Quint's next trainee class and a set of banging drums."

Her eyebrows go up.

I snicker at my unintentional pun and slide a hand into the back of her underwear from the bottom, cupping an ass cheek. "Sorry. The kind of drums you hit with a stick. They're not what I learned on, but hand drums aren't loud enough when everyone else is plugged in." I'm saying the words on autopilot —the rest of me is lost in the luscious sensations of her ass in my hand. I squeeze, letting my fingers dig into muscles that tense and then give way to the pressure.

Ari groans gently, so I move to sit between her legs and slide both hands into her underwear. I'll have to thank Chloe later—they're really stretchy. I use my thumbs to massage circles around her seat bones, which turns the groan into inarticulate gurgling.

I let my body drink in the sounds of Ari's pleasure. "Tell me something most people miss when they scene with you."

Her ass tightens in my hands.

I keep my thumbs working.

She chuckles ruefully and relaxes again. "That I'm a sucker for feathery touches."

My ego tries to escape its cage and billow around the room. I lock it down. This isn't about me. "Tell me something I missed."

She raises an eyebrow. "That's two questions, mister."

I let my thumbs slide into the valley of her pussy and back out again. "Fine. Ask your next one."

I see the brat light in her eyes before she speaks. "Tell me the one thing you've fantasized about doing to me that makes you hottest."

Hello, lethal. I slide my thumbs into the wetness of her pussy a second time. I need reinforcements for this one. Which almost backfires, because the slick heat of her is beyond distracting. "I want to slide into you while you're still asleep and have you wake up whispering my name."

Her entire body stills.

I don't walk it back. If I want her real and open, I need to show her mine.

She closes her eyes, and when she opens them again, there's a sheen of tears there. "Wow. Thank you."

There she is. I take a moment, my thumbs still, the rest of me barely breathing, to let us feel where we just landed.

Then I reach over and pick up the thing Quint calls a shrinkydink flogger. It's the one they entrusted us with first, and despite the annoying nicknames it's picked up, I know it's something I can't screw up. Which is exactly what I want right now, because all the tools I poured out on my floor are just decoration. This scene is mostly happening somewhere underneath our skins.

I trace the soft leather laces of the flogger along the sensitive skin of Ari's inner thigh. It's rapidly becoming one of my favorite curves.

She shivers again.

It's time to start learning how to turn that into quaking.

Chapter Twenty-Three

ARI

I feel my underwear sliding before I register what his hands are doing. Soft silk on the move, the lifting of my knees as he works them all the way off.

I open my eyes and watch appreciation light in his. He glides a finger lightly through my pussy, and then reaches for pillows, tucking them in as supports for my knees. He offers another bite of the earthy, redolent pastry I could totally be bribed with for the rest of forever, and then lifts me by my elbows, whisking my cami off before my lazy spine sinks me back into the pillows.

I grin at him, because clearly the man is no stranger to removing sexy underwear.

He grins back. "Comfortable?"

Any more so and I wouldn't need bones. "Yes."

This time the flogger brushes over my belly, so soft it feels like the silk he just slid off me. He flicks it, and the strands fall like soft rain.

Smart Dom. I like feathery impact play almost as much as I like feathery touch.

He's watching me with a focus I associate with really

skilled tops. I can tell he hasn't missed the changes in my breathing or the way my nipples have tightened.

I expect the flogger to move up, but it doesn't. He bends over and sucks one of my nipples into his mouth, hot and fast and hard. When he bites down, I nearly come all over his lap.

He chuckles, and then I feel a nastier bite. One that means he's just added a clamp, and he did it one handed, without looking, and fast enough he nearly caught his tongue in its teeth. I breathe into the fire. I love nipple clamps, but there's no way he could know that unless Harlan spilled way too many beans. I don't use them in public scenes. They fuck far too thoroughly with my control.

His mouth closes over my other nipple. This time, he tugs on the clamped one when he bites, and it's all I can do to hold my orgasm back.

He puts on the second clamp and cups me as he sits back up. "You don't get to come until I take these off."

Evil Dom. I give him the dirty look he's earned.

He swats my pussy, which just adds fuel to my wet fire.

He laughs and drums a freaking beat on my mound, hard and fast, and then picks up the flogger again.

Damn. He already has me riding the bleeding edge of orgasm, but I get smart and try to back off. No point advertising just how easy I am to torture.

The flogger lands on my thigh, and it's sharp enough to sting. I look into the eyes of my Dom and see the anger. "No hiding. Whatever else you do today, there will be no more disappearing parts of you out of a scene."

I stare at him, because he's calling me on bullshit he should absolutely be calling me on, but I can't believe he sees it. Nobody ever does. They trust my rep. Ari, all in, all the time.

Which used to be true, until putting all of me in every scene started to hurt too much.

He cups my cheek, and his touch is swampingly tender. "What don't you want me to know right now, beautiful?"

I don't know if we're still playing twenty questions or if this is just Dom instincts heading in for the kill, but either way, he'd have me in awe of his skills if I wasn't the prey at the end of his pounce. "I'm really close to orgasm, and I was trying to back off a little. This wasn't me trying to hide anything more than that. Just standard sub survival tactics. I don't want to make your job too easy."

He eyes me, weighing my words. "Okay. Your question."

He's got a really good poker face. I breathe, backing away a little further. Letting him see what I'm doing. He lets me go—my body, anyhow. The rest of me he's holding right here with his eyes. I swallow. "Why did you sit on a stool for three months before you asked me to play?"

"I sat in the dust for three years before I got to touch a drum. I knew I wasn't ready for you yet." He shrugs. "I'm still not, but you need me to get there faster than I was moving."

My breath catches in my chest. I knew the first part. I have no idea what to do with the sheer, wild arrogance of the rest of it—or how well he's seen into my soul.

He smiles and tugs on one of my nipple clamps at the same time as his fingers thrust up into my pussy.

It takes every bit of skill and pure, sheer stubbornness I have not to go over that cliff.

Chapter Twenty-Four

JACKSON

I didn't mean to edge her today. I know what my hands are good at, but I don't know her body all that well yet, and I expected to spend some nice, easy time hanging out with her on the lower rungs of arousal, figuring out what makes Ari tick.

At this point, I'm not sure she *has* lower rungs.

I look at the baby flogger lying over my leg and the toys sitting in my bowl and sigh inside my head. I wanted her to see that I'm not totally useless with the tools of this new trade, but it's hard to beat the delirious sensation of my fingers in her pussy.

I hold still, waiting for the fluttering around my fingers to stop. I've never actually seen someone fight off an orgasm like this, and it's an education.

Ari finally breathes out, and it's mostly a growl. I skim my thumb over her clit. She jumps and squeaks, which is so much fun I do it again. I don't recognize the language she curses in, but it's long and fierce and really inventive.

I chuckle and slide my fingers out of her pussy, letting

them trail up to her belly. "What's the longest time you haven't come for?"

Her eyes fly open, and I actually think I see fear there.

She doesn't know enough about me yet. I'm not into denial of pleasure. Not for more than a small part of an afternoon, anyhow. However, she hasn't answered my question. I wait and hope my Dom face does the work for me.

Her eyes go a little flat. "Almost two weeks."

I'm way more interested in the flatness than the number. "How are you feeling when you say that?"

She makes a wry face that mostly ends up looking unhappy. "Sad. Frustrated. I like to play hard, but I don't want to make new notches in bedposts just to make them."

I've heard the club Doms talking. Ari's a notch a lot of people want. Because she's beautiful, because she's skilled, because her confidence tends to ooze into everyone she plays with. "Notches aren't about you. They're about some idiot Dom's ego."

She shrugs. "It feels that way sometimes. Or I've just gotten too sensitive and I'm seeing things where they don't really exist."

I suddenly don't feel so bad about my beginner nipple clamps and grass tassels. There are no notches here today and this is absolutely not a competition. I bend over and nuzzle into the soft, lush valley between her breasts. "How are you feeling about me not letting you come right now?"

"Cranky." I feel the smile softening her words. "I somehow keep getting surprised by how well you read me."

I snort into the side of her breast and dart my tongue out for a lick around the edge of the nipple clamp. "I didn't expect you to be this responsive."

She makes a sound that says everything and nothing at the same time.

I reach my fingers for the clamp. "I'm going to take these off and I want you to hold absolutely still while I do. You don't get to come yet."

She whimpers, but nothing else moves. Which is insane—I tried the nipple clamps on myself once and they hurt like fuck coming off. I wait until she breathes again and lave the abused skin with my tongue. Then I turn my head and put my fingers on the other clamp. This time I remember some of Quint's instructions and slide my other hand between her legs.

She gets wetter when I take the clamp off.

I knew she liked some pain. Now I know she likes it from me.

I'm good with that. Pain for the right reasons is part of life. One of my proudest moments in Gambia was when Kengali had me play until my hands bled.

I give both of her nipples a little more affection, and then I sit up, letting two of my fingers slide back into her pussy. I tap them gently against her g-spot. Letting her know I'm there.

Then I wait.

She gives me a look. A distinctly grumpy one.

I tap her nose with my free hand. "You're earning things today, remember? Give me the orgasm I want first. Then you might get the one you want."

She glares at me and then at the baby flogger on my leg. "What about earning a chance to use the toys on you?"

Somewhere under the brat reply, we've just landed in serious. Serious that I've thought about, because she's a switch and that has some implications. But I'm pretty sure we need a better foundation before we go there. My gut says submission is the harder part for Ari. And while I don't think I have very many submissive bones, I might find it all too easy to let her lead.

We need to do the hard parts first. Find safe Ari can trust.

Even if we get there with some steaming bowls of water, Gambian pastries, and a flogger that belongs to a munchkin.

Chapter Twenty-Five

ARI

I've asked that question of a lot of Doms. I've never had one give me such clear-eyed, serious consideration.

I'm a switch. Most people aren't, or not enough of one to want to jump into the exponential confusion of playing on both ends of the power teeter totter. I don't think the man I'm looking at is a switch either, although I'm the first one to admit that he's blown up a lot of my preconceived notions about him in the last twenty-four hours.

But whatever his personal leanings are, he knows this matters to me. His silence isn't an answer—but it's respect.

I open my mouth to walk back the question and its snarky edges, and he smiles. "Not yet."

It takes me a moment to realize he just gave me an answer.

One that isn't no.

Holy fuck.

I blink at him, because I'm probably supposed to pull him aside right now and have a conversation about what a bad idea it is to try kinks that don't feel like yours and what a good idea it is to explore kinks that matter to your partner, even if they don't feel like yours on paper, which even I can hear is a conversation waiting to turn into a tangled knot from hell.

But I don't get to think about that for very long, because his fingers are doing their evil mischief in my pussy again, and my nipples are throbbing in response, and he's not giving me what I want at all, but ever so slowly, he's sliding me toward the orgasm I need more than my next breath.

I drop my overly chatty head down a deep well and let myself go into my body. The rest can wait. Right now I have a Dom who's entirely focused on my pleasure and I'd be the dumbest sub in the land if I let anything get in the way of that.

His fingers tap inside me again, a slow, lazy rhythm that makes me want to stab every drum he owns. He's pushing me up the slow, aching uphill of a roller coaster, the part that happens right before you get to the top—and I'm always the person who wants to get out and push.

Which is precisely why I don't wear latex all the time. Sometimes I need to be the one who isn't in control of the ride. I remind myself of that as I pant and try to wriggle Jackson's fingers a little deeper inside me without him noticing.

He growls, which is sexy as hell and also means I'm sucking at the stealth sub thing today. I open my eyes and try puppy-dog eyes instead, which only gets me a chuckle. He rubs his fingers in circles of torment inside me. "I can do this for a really long time, beautiful. You're not coming unless I decide you can."

I have no idea why I'm resisting him this hard. Most Doms don't look for my soft and gentle, but when they do, I'm happy enough to share. I frown at Jackson, suddenly needing to know the why I'm throwing up roadblocks. I'm getting in my own way, and I so very rarely do that.

He rubs a thumb over the creases in my forehead. "Stop thinking. Feel my fingers inside you. Feel their beat. Let it go where it needs to go." His hand travels down from my fore-head and starts tapping on my belly.

I've just become his drum, and something about that feels playful and light and full of sunshine, even if it's also making my all the blood in my body pool around his fingers.

His thumb brushes my clit and I hear the cymbal clang in my head. It doesn't keep clanging, though. This isn't a rock-and-roll-and-cymbals kind of orgasm he's building. It's slow and molten and it's no less hot for the lack of fireworks.

He presses down on my low belly, his fingers stroking from below. I grab the sparks and try to use them to throw myself over the top of the hill.

The beat stops. Entirely.

Dammit. The man is a freaking psychic.

I don't make him speak. I relax. Stroke the sparks wistfully and give them back.

He chuckles—and then, one molasses-slow inch at a time, he sends me over.

Chapter Twenty-Six

JACKSON

My fingers have just discovered their new life goal. They want time to stop while they hang out inside of Ari and play with the flutters of her orgasm as it flows into some kind of gentle standing wave that might never end. Which would be fine by me. The look on her face right now is as close as I've gotten to sacred in a really long time.

She comes back down very slowly, her eyes dazed and vulnerable and absolutely shutting off any more questions. I somehow thought we might do this a few times as we played our game. A way of building trust and laying down some of the train tracks of who I hope we can be.

She doesn't need tracks.

I work myself around her legs and into a reclining position on the pillows, facing her. I slide her legs up over mine, enjoying the feel of limp Ari. Satisfied Ari. I'm still playing with the toys they issue in kinky preschool, but we got somewhere good. Quint wasn't wrong about keeping it simple.

She turns her head so that her eyes are aimed at mine when she opens them. She smiles, and it's lopsided and happy. "That was nice."

Her voice sounds like an old jazz singer, the ones who smoked a couple of packs out back before they got up to sing. My ego isn't big enough to think I did that to her. Mostly she did it to herself, but she let me hold her cloak, and that feels damn good.

I trace a line down from her collarbone into the valley between her breasts, and then feather out, touching her nipples gently. They're still swollen, and I can see the marks the clamps left behind. "Tender?"

"Duh." She chuckles. "Ever worn those things?"

I shrug. "Only for a couple of minutes. Long enough to decide I was way too wimpy to be a submissive."

She reaches up a hand and threads her fingers through mine. "You tried them? For real?"

I'm not sure why she's surprised. "Sure. Quint said it's a good idea. I whacked myself with a crop some too. Paddles are kind of hard to aim."

Her smile is soft. "Not very many Doms bother."

I'm not going to lie here and let her give me extra credit for paying attention in class. I run my thumbs over her nipples again. "Tender, but okay?"

She nods. "Fine. And you're welcome to keep fondling them if you like."

I snort. This was a half-assed scene that's now turning into half-assed aftercare, both of which Quint would probably set on fire.

She grins as I slide a hand between her legs. "Or that."

I roll my eyes. "This is me checking to see that my dastardly actions left you in one piece."

She pushes up into my fingers a little. "Is that a really long way of saying I get my hard, fast orgasm now?"

Brat. "No." Which isn't the answer my fingers are voting for, but I learned in training class that Doms sometimes need to be patient and I'm beginning to understand why. There's magic in the space between what she wants and what I'm willing to give her. Magic for both of us. Bodies don't lie, and hers is happy, pliant goo.

Which I'm not nearly dumb enough to confuse with compliant.

She lets her fingertips trail over the hand that's cupping her breast. "Have I earned myself some more of those fried pastry things I need to know the name of before I leave?"

I laugh. The woman I buy them from will love Ari. "They're called akara. I'll hook you up with my dealer." I reach over to the plate and offer her another one, this time dipped in a sauce that's nothing but sweet. "Nibbles and a nap before you go?" It's really warm and cozy and nothing in me wants to move right now, but this isn't the part of the day I get to dictate.

She opens her mouth like a baby bird and snuggles in closer. "Yes, and yes."

Now for the harder question, and I want to get it out there before we take our nap. "Will you give me a week?"

I hear her sleepy brain snap back into gear. "Maybe. What do you have in mind?"

Simple. I hold up her panties. I'm about to become a kinky cliché and I don't care. "I don't want you wearing any of these. For the next week. Access, only for me, whenever I want it."

Her eyebrows fly up. "If you finger me in the grocery store, people are going to notice."

Fair enough. "Grocery stores are a hard limit, and anywhere else we might shock innocent vanilla bystanders. Any other places you'd like to have off limits?"

She opens her mouth to say something. Twice. And then just shakes her head.

I hide a grin. Being a cliché is fun. "How about sex?"

Her lips twitch. "You're leveling up fast."

Since she's currently got my cock pressed against her ass, I'm guessing she's not confused about why I'm asking. "Quint suggested I use the tools I have the most experience with."

She giggles, and it sounds like a freaking rainbow. "Cocks and drumsticks?"

Drumsticks hadn't even occurred to me. The inside of Ari's head must be a really awesome place. "Something like that."

She sighs and snuggles in. "No panties. In winter. Mean Dom."

I cup her ass and pull it in a little snugger. I need to give my cock a few crumbs. "Is that a yes?"

"Yes. One week. Exclusive. No scaring innocents, and your cock can go wherever it wants."

I kiss her cheek and grin. Those sound like the words of a shrewd negotiator, but her eyes and voice say she's half asleep and falling fast.

Clearly I scare her about as much as a litter of kittens.

I'll have to see what I can do about that.

Chapter Twenty-Seven
ARI

I should not agree to things while I'm half asleep.

I walk into the lounge where Quint and Scorpio are setting up and try not to look like I just got a surprise visit from their drummer. Between my legs. In the hallway.

It's not the easiest of walks because no panties when you're this aroused has some logistical issues. I surreptitiously adjust the waistband of the tight pants I wore to be a brat and sigh. Waving a red cape in front of even a baby Dom is generally a bad idea.

Quint catches the last of my adjustments and starts laughing. No words, just the belly chuckles of a friend who knows me really well and recognizes all the symptoms of tortured sub.

Scorpio rolls her eyes as I get closer. "Let me guess. Jackson got lost on the way to the bathroom."

Nothing about that man is lost at all. I'm pretty sure he could find my clit in the middle of Greenland in the dark. However, there are roles to be played here, and at least half of why I do this is my deep love of all the theater. "No idea. There are cookies in the kitchen. Maybe he took a detour."

Eli tilts his head at a plate. "What do you think we are, amateurs?"

Gabby has elevated cookie thievery in this joint to high art. Fortunately, I was here when she delivered the goods. Half of them are currently stashed somewhere no Dom would ever think to look. I march over and sit down in Eli's lap, mostly to keep them from thinking too much about what just happened in the hallway, and snag one of his cookies. "I think these are my faves." Gabby has some secret source for chocolate chips as big as your head.

Scorpio grins. "She says there are vegetables in these ones."

I give her one of the looks I save for delivery guys who think they get to cop a feel as their tip. "I wasn't born yesterday, sister."

"It's true." Eli breaks off half my cookie and somehow manages to get it to his mouth before I can stop him. "Pumpkin."

They are kind of orange. I eat the rest of the meager morsels he left me, because chocolate chips as big as your head trump vegetables any day of the week.

Scorpio breaks the last cookie in half and hands it to me. Sub solidarity. "She's testing recipes to get veggies into Evie. She says if we'll eat them, a picky two year old probably will too."

Evie has more will than any three Dommes I know. Her gramma, however, is no slouch, no matter what end of the teeter totter she might ride in the bedroom. "We're happy to sacrifice for science."

"You might save a few long enough for all of us to get a chance to sacrifice." Jackson's voice from the door is dry and amused and paired with a pouty face that puts Evie's to shame.

Scorpio walks over and brushes crumbs off his chin. "You take time to diddle your sub in the hallway, you lose."

I keep my eyes on my Dom, and I know everyone else on the stage is too. He's seen the teasing, but he's never been its target before. Some people don't hear the love at first, and if he's one of them, we'll need to walk it back.

Never mind the small issue of my ass currently in some other Dom's lap. I stay there. Some limits need to be felt in your bones before you know what they are. I might as well give his bones a chance to vote.

Jackson looks at Eli and grins. "Your keyboarding goes to shit when you have a sub in your lap. You might want to do something about that."

I grin and pop up. "I've never sat on a drummer before."

He tries, for one impossible second, to keep a straight face. Then he loses it, along with the rest of the band.

Eli swats my ass, which is well deserved, but he's far too amused to have good aim.

Quint just rolls his eyes. I stay out of arm's reach—I know he wouldn't miss.

Jackson picks up a drumstick and taps it on the inside of his forearm, a thoughtful look on his face. I back out of his reach too, because I'm not a sub who needs a lot of hints to know where my Dom's thoughts are going. "I have paperwork to do. And gear closets to organize."

Scorpio snorts. Quietly. She won't throw me under the bus, and if I'm really lucky, she'll keep the guy who wants to play rat-a-tat-tat on my ass busy enough that he doesn't come up with any more bright ideas before I manage to escape.

Jackson just smiles serenely. "It's good to know where I can find you."

Yikes. I make a mental note to stay really far away from the gear closets. Or to organize the cock-torture cupboard—it's excellent Dom repellent. "Leaving. Now."

I hear the high-five behind me and Eli's chuckle. "Nice Dom voice there, Jackson."

Scorpio growls at them all. "Focus? Please?"

I keep walking. And I grin.

Chapter Twenty-Eight
JACKSON

Having a woman with no underwear available round the clock is amazing. It's also work. Not because I mind touching Ari— that's about the last thing on Earth I'm ever going to complain about. But doing it in a way that keeps her off balance is trickier than I thought when I waved her lacy boy shorts around in my living room and casually tossed us into a week of serious immersion.

Immersion for me, at least. I have no idea what's going on in that head of hers when I'm not around, and so far there aren't a whole lot of people willing to rat her out.

Which means I forgot Quint's first rule and now I get to fry in the pan of not-simple.

I look down at the bag in my hand and walk into the yoga studio. I'm well aware this next thing I have planned will be pushing the limits we set, and it's going to be mostly up to Ari to make sure we don't scare any innocents. But I'm discovering one of the core truths of being a Dom. There's nothing quite as tempting as an inventive idea.

Jasmin looks up at me from behind the reception desk. "Hey, Jackson. I didn't know you were playing today."

Not the drums. "Just dropping by to pick up a couple of things."

Her attention is already dimming, shifting to the next cute guy walking in the door. "Sure thing."

Secure, this place isn't. I settle myself into a quiet corner to wait. Hopefully Ari won't pick this morning to sleep in.

About ten minutes before class starts, the door opens and she dashes inside, chased by a stiff wind off the lake. "Hey, Jasmin. Did you try that cookie recipe?"

The receptionist feigns a dead faint off her stool. "I'm going to get so much sex for those, girlfriend. My guy was ready to go down on me for a week."

This will teach me to hang out in shadowy corners. I step out far enough for Ari to see me and crook my finger before I learn anything else about what sexual favors Jasmin's guy is willing to exchange for baked goods. Which is probably a really weird position to take given what I have in my bag right now, but I never promised to be an intellectually consistent Dom.

Ari's eyebrows go up as she spies me, but that's all the reaction I get as she scans her card for the class and strips off her wet outer layers, hanging them on a hook in the forest of raincoats in the studio's foyer.

I let her take her time. All procrastinating will do is make her late for class, and it's fun to let her tangle herself up in her own rope.

I make a mental note to text Matteo about getting some rope lessons.

Ari ambles my way, just fast enough to keep a scowl off my face. "Fancy meeting you here, Sir. Are you drumming for my class?"

I take her hand silently and lead her into the skinny hallway that runs down the side of the studio. We pass a small kitchen and bathroom and arrive at a curtained-off room the owner uses for massage treatments.

I put a hand on Ari's back and push her gently into the dim, closing the curtain behind us. It has a polite message on the other side about treatment in progress, just in case anyone happens to wander back this way. It might even provide decent cover for a moan or two.

I give my eyes a moment to adjust to the shadows. I can make out the outlines of the massage table and the other trappings in the room, so I don't light the candle I left here as backup. Not quite a blindfold, but I'm going for a similar effect.

My sub is watching me, still and calm and ready. I haven't pushed her off-balance yet.

I step in close behind her and run my hands down her arms, collecting her wrists and bringing them behind her back. I loop the fabric in my hands around them several times. It's stretchy as heck, which makes for a good yoga headband and a crappy restraint, but I only need it to work for a few minutes. I run my hands down her arms again and take a step back. "Ass bare and bend over the table, legs spread as far as you can with your pants around your knees."

Chapter Twenty-Nine

ARI

Shit. I wince, because this scene just ran into a logistics problem and I don't want to have to say so. He's surprised me again, and even though I didn't drink nearly enough coffee to be ready for him this morning, this is really hot. I can hear the other people in my class slowly moving around the studio, rolling out mats, collecting blocks, assembling a blanket nest for opening meditation.

Orgasms are excellent meditation.

A low growl by my ear. "Now, beautiful."

Crap. The logistics issue hasn't miraculously resolved itself, and I'm pretty sure I can't shake my pants down my ass with hip wiggles alone. I brush my restrained wrists in the general direction of my waistband, hoping he'll twig to the problem. Pants down needed to happen before restraints, which doesn't sound like a big thing to fix, but baby Doms are really sensitive to screwing up and this one specifically asked me not to act like his trainer.

I can feel his attention on me, and his creeping doubt, wondering why I'm not following his really simple instructions.

Which I can't let grow and fester, because the rest of what he's set up here is totally in Ari's happy zone, and the last thing I want him to do is stop accosting me in semi-public places. I look over my shoulder and make eye contact so that he has something to fuss at me for if he needs to. "I might need your help with my pants, Sir." I watch his body language carefully. I need to know if I've just popped his ego balloon, because deflated Doms are high on my list of dangerous substances.

He gives me a quizzical look and glances down at my pants. At my bound wrists. I see when he gets it. The stillness. The small head shake. The gusty sigh.

Then he looks back up at me and the laughter in his eyes does something really important to my insides. "Not that bendy, huh?" I feel my pants starting to slide down my hips, aided by his warm hands.

Thank fuck. I wiggle a little, because he's going way too damn slowly and I'm pretty sure he won't spank my ass in here.

He chuckles in my ear. "Keep that up and I'm sending you in there wearing nipple clamps and weights."

Those would make downward dog interesting. I hold still, although I'm really pleased he's starting to think about toys that aren't on the beginner shelf. Scenes, too. He's pulled three of these feel-me-up stunts in the last twenty-four hours, and this one's a big step up from copping a feel in the storage closet during pink-drink-mix inventory. A big step up from the crop cupboard, too. Public makes everything way bigger, especially when obviously public is a hard limit. This is the first time he's tried to skate on the edges with me, and I can feel what it's doing to both of us.

I bend over as soon as my pants hit my knees, letting my face sink into the soft pad on the massage table. It's heated, which is a nice touch, maybe even an intentional one. I spread my legs, slowly enough to get his attention. I want him looking, even if this room is too dark for him to properly see the effect he's having on me.

His low groan tells me he's got other ways of knowing.

His fingers slide into my pussy, stroking the really clear evidence of just how aroused I am. I clamp my lips together. If this is when I finally get my hard orgasm, staying quiet is going to be a really big job.

His fingers play in my wetness a moment longer, and then I hear the unmistakable squelch of a lube bottle. I blink, because he totally doesn't need lube for where I thought he was going with this.

His hand slides up my ass crack, which comes bearing two more surprises. First, he's not tentative at all. And whatever he's spreading, it's not lube. Oil, maybe—which makes my trainer head rear up. Oil and most toys are a bad mix.

His hand settles on my shoulder. "Not a fuck-up. I promise."

Shit. Okay. He needs me to trust him, and really, the worst thing that can happen here is a butt plug that can't be re-used.

Butt plug. My sub brain finally catches up with what's going on. The evil man is going to send me off to yoga class with a plug up my ass. Which is a Dom cliché for a reason, and one I adore. I sigh happily and relax into the sheepskin under my cheek. I almost slept through my alarm this morning, and that would have been a real tragedy.

He chuckles and slides a finger in my ass.

I don't need this kind of warm up, but no way am I telling him that. Whatever oil he's using has an amazing, slick feel. Way better than lube.

His free hand moves in to hold my butt cheeks open, and I feel the cool, seeking presence of a plug. Not silicone, it's too cold for that. I relax under his hands. Nothing good has ever come from fighting the intrusion of objects into my ass, and he's finally stepping into one of my favorite kinds of play, so I want to make it as good for both of us as I possibly can.

He slides the plug in slowly, and I'm surprised by how big it is. Brave Dom. I can take it, but it's got enough girth to make the stretch fairly uncomfortable, and he's not being tentative about pushing it inside me at all. With some Doms I might suspect ignorance, but not this guy. I know who trained him on butt plugs, and Jimmy has a clear policy. If the sub isn't squirming, the plug isn't big enough.

A push that has me wincing, and then the plug is in place and my pants are sliding back up my ass.

I can feel my pouty face. I don't bother hiding it, because I assume the dark will do that for me, but I'm sad that he's ending it here.

He slides off whatever he's used to restrain my wrists and gives my covered ass a gentle pat. "Opening meditation has started. I set you up a mat and bolster in the back row."

My first thought—aww, that's really sweet.

Until my brain catches up with the vague something in his tone that isn't sweet at all.

Oh, shit.

Chapter Thirty

JACKSON

She's gorgeous, and easily the wiggliest meditator in the history of meditation. Also possibly the only one with a vibrator up her butt.

I grin and turn the thumb dial that will end the torture. For a while. I managed to find myself a good line of sight from the shadows, through the side door Athena kindly left open. This wouldn't be nearly so much fun if I couldn't see the results of tormenting my sub.

My sub.

Those two words send shivers up my backbone. Ari is my sub. For five more days. Which might worry some people, but it took me less than five hours to fall in love with the beat of a drum and spend the next six years of my life learning to be its worthy partner. If Ari and I are right, we'll know. A week isn't long enough to get there, but it's more than enough time to feel the rhythms of what could be.

Not that I'm taking much convincing.

I watch her, sitting tall on a bright-red bolster, legs crossed and hands calm on her knees, and marvel at the lithe, beautiful strength of her. I don't know if she was born knowing who she wanted to be, but her feet have been on a voyage of intense self-discovery longer than anyone I know, and the person she is shows the length and depth and breadth of her journey.

Kengali's village has a saying. "Blown clean by the hot winds." That's how you get wise. How you lose the weak parts of yourself and burn off the parts that don't belong and learn to keep precious water safely sequestered inside you.

It wasn't a saying that made a whole lot of sense until I spent my first summer in that valley.

Ari knows how to hold on to the water that matters.

Athena moves the class into some gentle stretches. This is mostly yin yoga, but it's hard to relax until you've gotten your limbs out of the shape of an office chair, and most of the people in here don't bend in all the ways the human body has been meant to go for thousands of years.

I rock my hips in the shadows, letting my energy move in the easy, cross-legged pose my body still assumes without thinking. Gambia didn't run to a lot of chairs. I wait for Ari to flow through a simple forward bend into a lunge. A squirmy one, so I stick to nice Dom territory and leave the vibrator off.

I can't resist once she hits downward dog, though. Ass in the air, heels down, hair flowing down to hide her face from most of the room. I turn the dial just enough to start the vibrator rumbling. I can't hear it—I picked the quietest one I could find, and Jimmy has the largest collection in the known universe to choose from. Fortunately, he likes to pass on his knowledge.

I'm under strict instructions not to take it past level three. Given how much the thing jumped in my hand on level two, it's not hard to imagine why.

Or why Jimmy nearly died laughing when I commented that it looked like a good choice for a beginner. It looks like sexy modern art, but apparently the last time he used its twin on Doxy, she refused to feed him for three days.

I inch the dial up a little more. It's probably a good thing I know how to cook for myself.

Ari's ass twitches, but she manages to flow into something resembling plank pose, and then into cobra. I catch the strange look Athena gives her, which tells me I've disrupted this particular flow quite enough. Athena probably doesn't strictly qualify as innocent, but I'm aiming to brush against the rules here, not dent them noticeably.

The playlist suddenly softens, the beat heading for something a lot more conducive to napping than to hatha flow. The class seems to take that as their cue, reaching for the mountains of bolsters and pillows and blankets that the average office-chair dweller needs to get comfortable lying on the ground. Ari's collection is fairly minimalist, but her work doesn't involve a whole lot of being trapped in one position all day, and when it does, Milo is the king of kinky ergonomics.

More wiggling and groaning as people get settled, and the room slowly settles into a lake of calm. A very quiet lake. I make a face. I was hoping the music was going to provide some cover for the continued torment of my sub, but I can practically hear Ari breathing.

Ah, well. Jimmy told me not to be a wimp. He said that's not what Ari needs, and he's right. She's done her time in the hot wind. A Dom who can't stand there with her should just pack up his drums and go home.

Chapter Thirty-One

ARI

I can't believe I thought he was cute.

Evil Dom. He's given up on making my ass vibrate forever, which was annoying enough. Now he's pulsing it. A few seconds here, a quick burst there. Random, mindfucking torture, and there's no way he doesn't know it.

I glare in the general direction of the open door, because I'm sure he can see me and that's the only place he could be, even if I can't spot him in the shadows. This place has way too many dark corners. We do that on purpose at Fettered, but here I'm pretty sure it's just the result of a lack of imagination.

I grit my teeth as my ass rumbles again. It's killing me to keep quiet, and not for the reasons most people would think.

I want to make noise. I want everyone in this room to hear. I live to push people out of their sexual comfort zones and into the big, wide world of pleasure, because so very many people could be happier than they are and have no idea what's possible. I'd be happy to come like a freight train right now and sprinkle happy, orgasmic, kinky pixie dust on everyone here.

But those aren't the rules.

The rules are that we leave the innocents lying peacefully on their bolsters and blankets and don't run any orgasmic trains into how they see the world. I can't believe I set a limit like that. All I really meant to do was rule out the grocery aisle.

Not because I think veggies are innocent. There's just no way eggplants aren't kinky.

My ass is back to being demented again, this time with short, sharp bursts that feel far too much like sex and drive all thoughts of eggplants really far away. Cocks are way better than eggplants, and Jackson moves like a guy who knows how to use his. Or can be taught. Whichever.

I green-lighted penetration. Which means it could happen.

I bite down on my favorite blanket, which is a mistake, because it's wool, which makes a really crappy gag.

Belatedly, I realize bodies are moving around me. Peacefully, in that slow, respectful way people have when they've almost fallen asleep. Clearly they weren't lying there thinking about some hard, fast anal sex bent over a massage table.

I groan, which sounds somewhat plausibly like I just woke up, and lever myself to my feet. I leave my nest of bolsters and blankets right where they are. I'll clean up later. I have a Dom to kill first.

He's waiting for me outside the door, leaning against the wall with his hands in the pocket of his jeans, looking like he picks up chicks outside yin yoga every day of the week. I walk over and nuzzle into his shoulder. "That was mean."

He chuckles. "What makes you think it's done?"

My massage table anal-sex fantasy leaps up and down, frantically waving its arms. "What would you like me to do next, Sir?" It's my politest sub voice. He probably has no idea just how infrequently I use it.

He wraps his arms around me, cuddling me tight, just like

the vanilla guy lounging around outside yin yoga might do. "You have work now, yeah?"

More or less. I have some party planning to go over with Gabby, and a drink-mix inventory to redo because I'm pretty sure my brain shouldn't be allowed to count things while Jackson is copping a feel. However, all those items could happily be pushed aside for massage-table shenanigans. "I can hang out for a bit if you like."

He drops a kiss into my hair. "Can't. I have a class to drum for over in West Seattle, but I'll drop by the club to see you later."

I snort into his sweater, which is really nice and fuzzy in all the right ways. "Is that a threat or a promise?"

He pats my ass. "This is staying in, so what do you think?"

I hesitate. I have fairly sensitive skin and it won't handle lube for hours.

His arms squeeze a little tighter. "I read your form. It's a stainless steel vibe and coconut oil. You'll be fine."

Evil, thoughtful Dom. And one who dropped a pretty penny on whatever he stuck up my ass.

Because he sees. Because he pays attention.

I close my eyes and cuddle in. He might think this week is about stripping my ass bare. I'm far too acutely aware of just how many other parts of me are beginning to feel naked.

Chapter Thirty-Two

JACKSON

I hold the door open for Gabby and shake my head at the plate of cookies in her hand. "Those are going to totally upstage what I brought."

She grins and slides two off the plate and hands them to me. They're still warm. This woman has crazy magic. "I came to thank Chloe for the special package she sent home with Daniel. Nobody makes lingerie for grandmothers."

I know other people tell her she's the sexiest grandmother they know, but that does grandmothers a disservice. Another lesson of Kengali's village. Women can be deeply erotic at any age, and any guy who doesn't support that is really dumb. Fortunately, Daniel isn't one of them. I take a huge bite of cookie and lean in to kiss Gabby's cheek. "Nobody makes cookies for bachelor drummers either, so thanks."

She gives me a smile filled with hints of devious. "I happen to know that Ari makes excellent cookies."

Villages don't keep secrets. They don't know the meaning of the word, especially when you're trying to romance the village sweetheart. "I'll do my best to be worthy of them."

That earns me a very curious glance at my bag and two

more cookies, which I hope is Gabby's way of saying that she approves. She heads off down the hallway to the kitchen. I stand where I am and eat. I'm smart enough not to walk into the lounge with three uneaten cookies in my hand.

Which is how I look like a five-year-old boy when Ari rounds the corner.

She takes one look at me and cracks up laughing. "Let me guess. You know Gabby is here."

I grin, because there's no point telling lies when there are cookie crumbs on your face. I hold out the single cookie I haven't gobbled yet.

She breaks off half and backs away a step as she nibbles it, eyeing me warily. "Band practice isn't for an hour."

Smart sub. "Keeping track of where I'm at, are you?"

She snorts and wiggles her ass. "There are reasons."

I've was tempted to walk around the block and see what the range on the remote was like, but I'm discovering that I like seeing the results of my work up close and personal.

I reach into my bag, enjoying her small tremor. Not quite nerves—more like quivery anticipation. Causing that is something I could get used to really fast.

I pull out a small paper bag, which was the closest my apartment ran to wrapping paper. "I brought you a present."

Her eyes light up, and I bless, yet again, the wisdom of learning with your eyes first. Ari loves presents. Lives for them, goes totally gooey nuts for them—and somehow most people don't seem to know that. People often bring her things, but it's cookies or the latest sex toy they found. She appreciates those too, but she already seems to know this is something more personal.

I take her hand and lead her over to a small bench under a window. I want light for this, and Seattle has actually managed to produce a few sunbeams this afternoon. Even the skies are on my side.

I sit her down and hand her what looks like a lunch bag. The effort went into what's inside, and watching her hold it, stroking the creases in the simple brown paper, is suddenly making me very nervous. I'm not sure either of us are ready for what's inside.

She's not tentative when she opens the bag. She dives in like a kid who just had to wait ten years for Christmas, and gets the contents all the way out before they register.

Her breath catches, and I have a horrible moment of wondering if I've pushed way too hard—and then she exhales, and it's a sound of soft, pure, shocked delight. Her finger reaches out to touch the woven fabric I painstakingly sewed onto a set of boring black leather cuffs. "Jackson." A whisper. One that sounds full of tears.

I wait. If I've watched well enough, she'll see all the layers.

She looks at me and her eyes nearly swamp me. "This is like your bag. The beautiful one."

The one I made in Africa that she touches every time she sees it. "It's cloth that I wove around the same time. It was supposed to be a strap for the bag, except it took six months to make this much and I was going to die before it was long enough to be a strap."

Her fingers trace the intricate pattern work that has more of my blood, sweat, and tears in it than anyone would ever assume from looking at it. There was literally a half inch left when I finished stitching it onto the cuffs. Somehow, the leather took my unsteady, drunken weaving and turned it into something amazing.

Her finger moves to the leather, tracing the top edge of one of the cuffs. She looks at me again, and this time, there's something deeply vulnerable riding in her eyes. "These are my favorite cuffs."

Someone has not given this woman enough presents. "I know." I probably could have asked any Dom in the club and found out, because that's the kind of detail people here pay attention to, but I watched. These are the model she picks for herself every time. "I oiled them, but they might be a little stiff yet."

Chapter Thirty-Three

ARI

He's just entirely overwhelmed me. Again. He's got a wild talent for it. I lean into him, needing the contact. Needing him to wrap around my softness, because I have a question and it's not going to be an easy one for either of us but I need to ask, because he's a baby Dom and it's entirely possible he doesn't know what he just did. What a pair of cuffs from a Dom to a sub usually means.

I swallow and tip my eyes up to meet his. "They're beautiful, Jackson. Tell me what they mean."

He smiles. "More than we're maybe ready for. Less than what I think you just got worried about."

I push off his chest a little. Baby Doms aren't supposed to be this good at mind-reading. "Say more about that, sexy, confusing man."

He grins. "I don't mind confusing you."

I make a face. "Duh."

He laughs, which gets him so many bonus points. So many. He likes me goofy, and that's such a part of who I like to be, even in the deeply intense moments. Which this one is, even though my insides are doing their very best to turn into warm caramel.

He frees up a hand to stroke my hair. "There are no strings. No expectations." He pauses and kisses the top of my head. "I wanted you to have something that's a part of me. It felt right."

He sewed me freaking cuffs with his own hands. Cuffs my covetous self wants on my wrists right this minute. Cuffs that for most people would be the kinky equivalent of asking me to go steady at the very least. And I can feel, deep inside me, that I would welcome that. Which is fairly earth-shattering news. I back away again just enough to get a good look at his face and blurt out the last thing that really matters. "We haven't had sex yet."

He laughs, and it shakes some of the cookie crumbs off his chin. "Is that a prerequisite to giving you presents?"

I shake my head. "No. Sorry, that was a really dumb thing to say."

His tucks my hair behind my ear. "I've been watching you for a long time, Ari. It's okay if you're not where I am, or if you never get there. These are a gift, straight out."

They're a magnificent one. They're exquisite and they're totally me.

I breathe out. He's not attaching any strings—but my insides just did. "I'd like to take that week we agreed to and make it open-ended. See if we can grow into whatever this is."

His eyes close. "Wow. Thank you."

I cuddle in close again, because this time we both need it.

His hand strokes my hair, soft and worshipful and soothing. "I don't know exactly what that means with your work here."

I manage a strangled laugh. "Believe it or not, I don't know either." Exclusive isn't really a thing I do. "A lot of that depends on what you're comfortable with. I know how to have my heart in one place and my pussy in many, but I'm not saying that's how this has to go."

He breathes out. In. "I know you're a deep part of the fabric of this place, and I'm not asking you to pull out of it. I've been watching you scene with other people for months, and I've walked myself through most of the bullshit I was carrying around that."

This man is a gift as exquisite as his cuffs. "I didn't know." Which is shocking. It's not boasting to say that I know everything that goes on in this place. Most days it's just simple truth.

I feel his chuckle more than hear it. "I worked pretty hard to make sure you didn't."

The lack of ego in that is astounding. And the sacrifice. I know what I do at the club. Watching couldn't have been easy, no matter how many vanilla preconceptions he talked himself out of while he sat on his stool and drummed. I've spent my whole adult life riding the sharp edge of personal growth. I'm beginning to realize I'm looking at a man who's made that same commitment at least as deeply as I have.

Which means I'm going to let go of some things that normally feel pretty important to me. Not because he's asked. Maybe because he didn't. "I need to be able to keep running training sessions and demos, but there are lines I can draw. Tell me what makes you most uncomfortable to watch."

His eyes are dark and steady. "This isn't about making me comfortable."

Stubborn, beautiful man. I hold up the cuffs. "Tell me when you would want me to take these off."

I can see that hit him in the gut. "I don't want to make you smaller, Ari. I don't."

Baby Dom. Brave and wise and still so very new to my

world. "Limits don't make me smaller. Not if we set them for the right reasons. I need to know, Jackson. I'm about to draw some lines here, and I can guess, but they'll be better lines for both of us if you tell me the truth."

He laughs a little. "Feet, meet fire."

I tap his cheek because he's adorable and I want to gobble him like Gabby's cookies.

He nods and swallows. "I had to walk away from watching you have sex. Which probably makes me a possessive thug."

About damn time. "No sex with other people. That goes both ways. Keep talking."

He doesn't look all that reassured yet. "You giving other people orgasms is okay, I think. Especially in a training context."

That would trip up a lot of people. It isn't what's scraping on him, but something still is. "But?"

He grimaces. "I'm trying to get my words right. I want to say that you coming for other people is hard, and it is, but some times are worse than others for me."

This man has more ability to look unflinchingly in the mirror than almost anyone I know. I stay quiet and let him look.

He nods again, his face relaxing. He's sorted something out. "The hardest ones are when you're not all there. When you're backing away or in trainer mode or you're the submissive in the scene but you're not really submitting. When you can't, because the Dom is too new or too clueless or hasn't figured out that he needs to push you harder."

Dots line up really fast and draw a crystal-clear picture. "That's why you've been such a hard-ass when I try that with you."

He nods slowly. "I think those times make you smaller."

All the air leaves my chest. "They make me bigger too. It matters to me to help people learn."

"I know." His eyes don't leave mine. "But it's the part where you get smaller that's hard for me to watch."

When this man gets all his skills down, he's going to be one fucking scary Dom. "Okay. No orgasms for me. No sexual touch where I'm the recipient."

He shakes his head fiercely. "That's not what I need."

Fierce, exquisite, beautiful man. I cup his cheeks. "It's what I need, Sir."

He stares at me.

I let him see just how vulnerable I am in this moment. "I know. I'm the chick who pushes all the edges and kicks possessive-guy crap in the knees."

He leans his forehead into mine, eyes wry. "Yup."

And he was prepared to let me keep being that. "This is what I want. For me. It feels really nice that it lines up with what will be more comfortable for you, but this is about me. I'd like to hold the intense sexual energy between us for a while. See where it goes."

He breathes out slowly.

I take his hands. "I touch other people and make them come, and I'd like to keep doing that in a demo or trainee context, because it's a really important part of what I do here. But I want you to know that isn't the same experience for me. It's not impersonal, but it's not the same as what's happening between us, even if it might look similar on the surface."

He chuckles. "I've seen what you do to some of your subs. They're very brave people."

My insides melt a little more. I grin, totally pleased he's watched my Domme scenes too.

And somehow, no longer surprised.

Chapter Thirty-Four

JACKSON

Damon pours a glass full of pink and pushes it down the bar at me. "So how many people have threatened to kill you so far?"

I raise an eyebrow and take a sip. Clearly I don't have enough sugar in me to make sense of this conversation yet.

Harlan steals Damon's drink, which isn't pink. "You're chasing the woman most of us consider a little sister, and some of us are dumb enough to think she might need protection."

My brain catches up. Fast. "In that case, Quint is in line ahead of the two of you. And probably Mattie and Sam, although they haven't said anything and they wouldn't bother using something as simple as their fists."

Harlan contemplates his knuckles. "There's something to be said for a good, simple fist."

I manage not to snicker. Harlan's a big teddy bear. "Scorpio will be mad if you hurt her drummer."

He snorts. "If you hurt Ari, Scorpio will get to you long before I do."

I down half my drink. "If you guys are done with the intimidate-Jackson part of the program, I'd appreciate any advice you might have."

Damon's grin at Harlan is wry. "Told you so."

Harlan shakes his head at me. "You're supposed to be pissed off and growling at us right now."

That would be a total waste of air. I can't imagine two guys less likely to be scared off by bear noises. "I'm supposed to be a lot of things. The only one I'm interested in is being a better Dom."

Harlan just grunts.

Damon raises his glass my way. "From what I've seen, we probably won't need to revoke your membership."

I manage not to roll my eyes. They're like a tough-guy comedy routine. "Does this shit work on most baby Doms?"

He grins. "Yup."

Harlan claps me on the back. "Quint says you handle her well and you learn fast and he might not have to set you on fire. I haven't seen anything to make me disagree with that. Scorpio thinks you're good people, and I don't disagree with that either."

Good people and good enough to be Ari's Dom are two very different things and we all know it. I empty my glass and try again. "Any advice?"

He nods. "Yeah. Don't listen too hard to old-fart Doms who think they know everything. You've got good instincts. Trust them."

Damon shakes his head and refills my glass. "This old-fart Dom thinks you should sign up for lessons with every person who has a skill you want to acquire."

I blink at him. That's not what I expected to hear. "You think I need to do that to keep up with her?"

He chuckles. "No, actually." His eyes shift to dead serious. "If you have a weakness, it's that you assume your lack of skills means you're not good enough for her. And she's got that same weakness because too many baby Doms have seen her as a trophy instead of as a human being with more soft spots than she lets most people see."

Harlan nods. "Good catch, boss."

Damon is still looking at me, and in the depths of that look rides the guy I've heard about. The one who made a safe space for kink in this city and did it without ever raising a fist. "If you two don't make it, I want it to be for the right reasons. Not because she's holding too tight to her idea that a baby Dom can't take her where she needs to go. Or because you let her hold on to that."

My breath huffs out. "I'm doing my best to convince her otherwise."

The steel hasn't left his eyes. "Sometimes what a sub believes can change through experience. Sometimes you have to crack it over the head with a hammer." He gives me another long, thorough study. "Don't be afraid to use a hammer if you need to."

I raise a wry eyebrow. "You're suggesting I use a hammer. On Ari. With half the club waiting in the wings to kill me."

Damon grins, and it's really clear why he's one of Seattle's top predators. "Yes."

Harlan claps me on the back. "This is not a job for wimps."

Or for people who want to keep breathing. But it might still be really great advice. I look over at Harlan, because I might as well keep asking questions while I have two of the best Doms in Seattle riding my ass and trying to prop it up at the same time. "How do you balance the soft and the hard? As a Dom, and in what you ask of your sub?"

"Shh." His head tries to disappear into his shoulders. "Don't say that too loud or Scorpio will maim both of us."

Damon snickers.

Harlan gives him the evil eye. "Just because your sub is all ladylike and gentle, don't think she won't kill you in your sleep."

Damon grins. "Answer his question, asshole. Or I will."

Harlan rolls his eyes, but when he looks at me, he's gone somewhere serious. He leans forward, intent. "You trust. You watch. You listen to that little voice inside you that doesn't always make sense but is usually right. You've already figured out that Ari needs soft, even if she doesn't always want it, and that puts you way ahead of most of the jerks who want to play with her."

They don't get to play with her anymore. Not until Ari and I figure this thing out or blow it up, and there's something really strong and bendy and good in knowing that.

Harlan blinks. "Holy shit—you got her to go exclusive?"

I stare at him, and then at Damon.

Damon smirks. "If he wasn't managing my club, he'd be a really rich psychic."

Harlan punches him, and it doesn't look gentle. "Shut up, asshole." Then the big guy looks at me. "That means you really matter to her. She doesn't do that."

Somewhere in this comedy routine, they've pointed me toward a lot of solid ground, and I hope they can see that in my eyes. "She does now."

I'm somehow not surprised to find Scorpio lurking in the shadows as I head back to the private rooms to check on gear setup. I'm only surprised Eli isn't with her. He might look like an elegant, easygoing guy in a suit, but I've seen the band together. They're tight, and while I think they underestimate Jackson a lot less than I do, they're still going to close ranks around him.

Her eyes zoom straight to the cuffs on my wrists. "Are those what I think they are?"

It's Scorpio. She might be here as Jackson's fierce older sister, but she's my friend too. I let her see some of what's still swimming in my eyes. "Yes."

She reaches out a finger to touch them, which I suspect is going to happen pretty often. "They're freaking gorgeous."

They are, but that isn't why she's here. "Spit it out, tough girl. I know you want to."

She grimaces and looks at me, her finger still tracing Jackson's weaving. "I know you and Mattie have a thing about baby Doms."

We have reasons. "Same as you would about amateur guitar players crashing your band."

Horror flashes in her eyes.

I press my advantage, because this friend doesn't blink often. "They might have hot skills, but they don't know how to play well with others or how to read the nearly invisible cues that flow between band members or when to stop being a hotshot and ride the magic of what you've created together, right?"

She nods slowly. "Okay, I get it, although I feel compelled to say that I was pretty damn green when Harlan decided to stick his hands down my pants."

That story has turned into one of Fettered's urban legends. People take pilgrimages to the stone wall where the big guy first rocked her world. "You and Emily and Meghan too. But it's easier when the greenie is the sub."

She makes a face, but she nods. "Yeah. Or the piano player, or second guitar." She gives me a look laced with empathy. "Way harder if it's the drummer, though. Lose the beat and the whole song goes to hell."

I give her what I can. "He's a really unusual baby Dom. He's got skills most of them don't have. Some from the music and some from the life he's chosen to walk."

She sighs and steps in, laying her head on my shoulder. "But you're not convinced yet."

"I can't be." My words are soft, because she's not riding my ass now—she's trying to help it stay afloat. "It's not just about protecting my heart, although I'm allowed to do that. It's about not putting too much pressure on this before we're ready."

She pushes off my shoulder and laughs. "That's bullshit. You know that, right?"

I kind of don't. I stare at her, because Scorpio says it straight, every time. Unless there's sexy lingerie involved.

Her face gentles. "Either he can handle you or he can't, Ari. Neither of you are going to know unless you go all in."

I raise an eyebrow. "You underestimate his Dom skills if you think he's letting me half-ass scenes."

Scorpio's face runs through a movie of expressions, all of them priceless. "I don't think I want to know that about my drummer."

I laugh. "You saw your second guitar player thoroughly fuck his barmaid two nights ago. Your band has sex, sweetie. You're going to have to deal. Even if you mostly think of Jackson as your kid brother."

She scowls. "The others were big, scary Doms before I met them. Jackson's got this innocence, and I want to keep him shiny."

I keep my mirth from hooting down the hallways, but it's a near thing. "He's the drummer in a sex-club band. If you want him shiny, you need to go play church gigs or something."

This time I get the look that says Scorpio could be a deadly switch if she wanted to be. "That's just mean."

"I know," I say quietly. "Which is why Jackson can't be shiny if he wants to play with me."

"Maybe." Scorpio's silent for a long time. "Look, you've got a bunch of assumptions about who can keep up with you, and they're mostly not wrong. It's good to keep your ass covered." She reaches out and touches my cuffs again, and this time her eyes are sad. "But Jackson's a guy with some really interesting depths, and you're going to fuck him up if you play that game."

I was wrong. His band underestimates him just as much as I did. "I repeat, he's a better Dom, and a more demanding one, than you think he is." I shrug and make a face, because she's the last person who expects me to be perfect. "He's surprising the fuck out of me."

Scorpio's smile takes a while, but when it arrives, it's full of wicked delight. "Go, Jackson."

I'd be jealous of his cheering squad, except I know darn well they're cheering for both of us. "Give us space, okay? I hear you. I have some preconceived notions about baby Doms that could do us harm, and I'm used to controlling the pace and depth, maybe a little too much."

Scorpio snickers.

I roll my eyes. "That wasn't innuendo."

She walks away, shaking her head. "Don't mess up my band."

I watch her go, my fingers sneaking toward the weaving on my cuffs again. I told Scorpio some of the truth of Jackson as a Dom, but not all of it. I don't know how to say the rest yet. He was so sweet when he put the cuffs on. So touched. So freaking tender.

I know he's got steel in him, but that's mostly not who he is with me.

I ignore the voice in my head that thinks that might be a problem. It hasn't been yet, and it's long past time I got done making assumptions about what Jackson can and can't be. I need to see. There's a really good chance this will crash and burn, and a lot of it will be because of the person I need to be, but I'm not going to crash it with bad driving inside my own head. Driving Scorpio just called out, because that's what kinky friends do for each other. I need to take all my labels off Jackson, and all my labels off me, and see what happens.

I sigh. I know part of the problem is that I'm feeling lonely lately. Vulnerable. Scared I've turned myself into someone really hard to partner. I'm not feeling like the Ari I mostly try to be, the one who can bloom wherever she lands.

The plug in my ass buzzes.

I lean against the wall and shake my head, stupidly amused despite all my best intentions. The man has uncanny timing.

I listen, but I don't hear footsteps in the hallway. My Dom isn't coming for me, not right this moment, anyhow.

Maybe it's time I go find him.

Chapter Thirty-Six

JACKSON

I'm pretty sure she walked in here just to exact a little revenge. She's busied herself with something behind the bar, but given the dirty looks Quint is firing, she isn't supposed to be back there.

She hasn't given me any looks at all. I'm Dom wallpaper, something she's so used to in her world that she's just bopping along to the beat of whatever's playing in her headphones.

I pick up the beat I can see in her body with my drumsticks. Eli and Quint are still screwing around with our set-up, but drums have never needed amplifiers, so I'm superfluous for now. I can sit on a stool and enjoy the heck out of the woman who has agreed to be mine for a while.

I don't let myself get stuck on the last two words. In Gambia, I learned to treat time loosely. To not get so stuck on beginnings and endings that I forgot to be in the middle. Ari and I aren't quite at the middle yet, but we're past our beginning, and that feels really good.

I take my hands to a simple beat and ponder what I might do next, here in this interesting middle. Mostly I've been running scenes I'm sure I can keep under control, ones so short they probably don't even qualify as real scenes. Kinky snippets where I know what I'm doing and nothing has much of a chance to go off the rails. Baby sessions that fit the Dom I'm going to be for a while yet, especially when the woman I want to be with has spent a solid decade of her life climbing the rungs of this particular ladder.

But it isn't a short scene I want right now, or a simple one. She's wearing my cuffs, and she keeps looking at them and going all melty, and that's doing something primal to the beat inside my cock.

He's done with waiting.

I shake my head and grin. He's not a romantic. More of an action man.

I put down my drumsticks and step off the stage. I can feel Quint's eyes on the back of my head, but I don't care. One baby Dom, taking himself off the leash. My sub is waiting for me and I know what she needs, or I'm going to stick with the arrogance of that until it thwacks me upside the head and says something different.

She doesn't look up my whole walk to the bar, which has to be intentional. Nobody sneaks up on Ari, not when there's only four of us in the lounge and my footsteps sound like I'm wearing combat boots.

I growl a little when I get close and her eyes fly up.

Better. I don't want to be someone she can ignore. I stride around one end of the bar, in behind the counter. As I pass her, I wrap my fingers around one of the cuffs. I keep walking. She'll catch up.

I hear a quick inhale as she scrambles to follow me. "Well hello, Sir. Nice you dropped by. Where are we going?"

Sometimes the brat needs attention. Sometimes she needs to know that she doesn't get to win. I head out the other end of the bar and take a sharp right turn into a small square area, fenced in on three sides by walls and swinging doors. I reach Ari's wrist up the wall and engage one of Milo's seriously awesome magnetic toggle switches.

My sub gulps as her second wrist joins the first. She tilts her head back and scowls at the hook I've just attached her to. "That must be Quint's fault."

Probably. He does enjoy torturing his barmaid. And this little nook is out of most major sight lines without being remotely private. I wrap my fingers around Ari's wrists, molding my body to her back. Absorbing the riot of sensations as she leans into me, letting her weight rest on her wrists and my cock.

I don't worry about her wrists—she knows what she's doing in restraints. I'm far more interested in her body language. There's no fight in her, no resistance. Only softness.

I grin. It's taken days to get there, and that's totally not what I want from her right now. I run my hands down her arms and glide over her ribcage until I've got two luscious breasts in my hands. I tweak her nipples through the thin fabric of the gauzy top she's wearing, hard enough to have her gasping.

I tug the stretchy fabric off one of her shoulders and bite her neck as I grind my cock into her ass. One hand travels down to the short red skirt she's wearing and discovers it isn't stretchy at all. Which means it needs to go. I unzip it and let it fall to the ground. Then I back away from her, because I have some logistics to take care of.

I kneel down, running my hands down her legs as I go. She's wearing garters, which I've never actually seen in real life before. Red lace running down to red stockings, which need to stay on, because my eyes totally deserve this gift—and because I have no clue how to get them off.

I lift one of Ari's feet, clad in a sexy red ankle boot, and step her out of her skirt. Then I put her foot up on a block. It looks deceptively simple, but I know Milo engineered the heck out of these things. Padded, stable and non-skid—guaranteed not to dump a sub on her ass, no matter what.

Really useful when you're six inches taller than the woman you're about to fuck.

Chapter Thirty-Seven

ARI

It takes longer than it should for me to realize what's just happened. He sucked me in with those slow, gentle demands of his, and now he's caught me totally off guard with one of the oldest Dom tricks in the book. One I'm really struggling to accept is connected to this Dom.

I look down as he taps my other ankle, cuing me to shift my weight. There's only one reason I can think of that he would be putting me up on blocks, and it just does not compute.

He looks up and grins at the shock that must be on my face. "Hello, beautiful. I hear we haven't had sex yet. About time we fix that, don't you think?"

I gape. He just strung me up on a hook on the wall beside Quint's bar where his whole damn band will hear whatever happens next. I don't ask him if he's sure. I read body language as well as anyone, and there's no doubt in him.

He wants this just as much as when he makes me come like a marshmallow.

Freaking sneaky Dom. He had me believing he was all sunshine and lollipops. Me. Who's been at this at least ten times long enough to know better. I feel the laughter trying to shake my ribs, and I let it out, because there's just no holding it back.

He slides his way back up my body and tweaks my nipples. "What's so funny?"

I shake my head, hoping he can hear the ruefulness in my voice. "You totally got me. I so wasn't expecting this."

His growl is low and damn fucking pleased with himself. "Good."

I break every sub rule in the book. "Why?"

He bites my shoulder again as he toggles the switch that will move the hook up the wall and take away the slack the blocks have made. "Because this is easy for you."

That would be his steel talking. And my answer. This is my reward for giving him my marshmallows. I lean into the cuffs and grind back into his cock, because he hasn't told me I can't yet, and I intend to drink every drop of this he'll let me have.

He chuckles and swats my ass. "You can do that when my cock's inside you. Until then, you wait patiently."

I'm many things, but patient has never been one of them. I try to keep my groans quiet—it won't take much for his band to consider my noises an invitation, and I don't know whether the guy sliding his fingers into the slick of my pussy actually intends for us to have an audience.

I hear footsteps. Measured ones. Quint, coming over to the bar. Trying to clue Jackson in, most likely.

Two fingers slide into my pussy from behind, and Jackson's breath closes in on my ear. "If he hears you come, this is your last hard orgasm for a week."

That's evil. I hate being quiet and he knows it. He's also smart enough to leave me with choices. I grit my teeth and remind myself that marshmallow orgasms aren't so bad.

His fingers rap a beat on my g-spot that nearly sends me straight through the roof—blocks, hook, cuffs, and all.

He chuckles and pulls his fingers out, snapping the strap of my garter as he goes. "Doesn't look like you need much of a warm-up, beautiful."

He's had a freaking vibe up my ass all day. He has about ten seconds before I come. I groan as quietly as I can and bite my bottom lip. I really want his cock inside me before I go over.

I hear the rip that can only be a condom package, and then he's right where I need him, cock lined up straight at my pussy and his hands on my hips. I breathe in sharp, whispered whimpers. I need this. Hard and fast and straight in and please don't let him think I'm fragile.

His fingers tense on my hips and then he's balls deep inside me in one arrowed thrust.

The sound that breaks loose from me probably earns me marshmallow orgasms until I'm thirty, but I don't care. The sheer rightness of what just happened in my pussy is entirely, utterly worth it.

Chapter Thirty-Eight

JACKSON

No words. There are no words for how this feels. The wet heat of her clamped around me and every cell of her body screaming its clear, uncensored delight. Mine too. We're two people who absolutely want something, arriving there together.

Loudly.

I make a face and scan what of the club I can see, because clearly my scene-management skills have failed me again. I don't care what people can hear, but I don't want anyone coming to look over my shoulder.

The only person in sight is Quint. He's looking straight at my reflection in the mirror of his bar, grinning his ass off as my sub freight trains toward her first orgasm loudly enough that people on the street probably know what's going on in here.

Ari moans again and lets loose an entirely illegal wiggle. One my cock is totally on board with allowing.

I give up caring what Quint or anyone else can see and put all my attention where it belongs. I'm deep inside the woman I've been watching for months, and there were a lot of moments when I didn't think this would ever happen.

I wrap an arm around her ribs, pulling her back tight against my chest. The blocks have her at the perfect height for this, and I thrust in again, my other hand using the wall for leverage.

She keens, and I can hear she's riding the high, thin edge.

I'm not going to make her wait this time. I jackhammer three quick, intense thrusts straight into her g-spot and grin as her edge totally blows up. I can hear my noises joining hers, but I yank my edge back. I'm not going over yet, no matter how tempting it is.

I back off on my thrusts just enough to let the pieces of her settle back down onto the cliff. She's panting, and her shoulders are covered in a sheen I lean down and lick. She sags against me, and I chuckle and tweak her nipple. "I'm not done with you yet, beautiful. Keep those legs working for me."

I follow my words with a rapid-fire series of thrusts, changing the angle up just a little so new parts of her get to play.

She moans and rubs her chest against the arm that's doing wall support.

I need more limbs. That's the one that's trying to keep us from doing a face plant.

Ari's forearms settle against the wall, as if she's read my mind. Maybe she has—this isn't her first handcuffed-to-a-wall rodeo. I move both hands up to her gorgeous, needy nipples and pinch, hard enough to have her yelping. My cock joins in on the action from below.

Ari's back arches, a woman desperately trying to be two places at once. I roll her nipples one at a time, keeping rhythm with my cock in her pussy.

Her wail is a primal, gorgeous thing. This time she doesn't bother teetering on the edge. She incinerates it. Her pussy clenches hot and wild around me and it takes everything I have not to go to ashes with her.

We're panting in unison now. Hot, ragged breaths that share what little oxygen is left in our tiny square of the world.

I don't let her come down much this time. I want one more from her. I reach into the pocket of my shirt. I have one trick left, and I'm pretty sure it's going to wreck any self-control I have left.

Chapter Thirty-Nine

ARI

I feel his hand leave me, but nothing about that processes. Not until my ass starts vibrating, anyhow.

His fingers come back to my nipples, and then he jerks and lets loose a long, vicious growl.

I can't stop the giggles. He's blown me wide open and there's nothing I can do to stop them. So I revel instead, in the knowledge that my Dom has just fucked himself at least as thoroughly as he's fucking me. Dom cock, meet evil vibrator.

A hand lands on my thigh, not at all gently. "This is the last hard, fast orgasm you get until you're wrinkled and gray, beautiful. Are you really going to spend it laughing?"

Possibly, but that's not going to do this next orgasm any harm. It's coming for me like a hot, angry avalanche, and everything in me wants to meet it head on.

One more eye-tearing twist of my nipples and Jackson puts one hand back on the wall and the other between my legs. His cock beats hard time into my pussy and the vibe takes that fire and spreads it everywhere.

I open all of me to what's coming. His fingers squeeze my

clit just as the avalanche slams home, and I tilt back my head and let go an incoherent howl of victory.

He thrusts hard enough to split me in two and his howl joins to mine. I feel him pulsing inside me right before I'm no longer capable of feeling anything at all.

I'm not sure how long it takes me to have a functioning brain again, but when I do, we're in a pile at the bottom of the wall, my legs tangled inelegantly with his, his breath hot in my ear. I bless Milo's quick-release genius—the kind that leaves the cuffs on my wrists, because even cross-eyed with pleasure, I'm already moving my fingers to feel them.

Or trying to, anyhow. I officially have limp noodles now instead of arms.

Jackson chuckles and runs his hands down my spaghetti limbs. "Anything hurt?"

I do the check-in, but I know I'm high enough on endorphins that nothing will register for a while yet. "No."

His fingers move to my ass, which is when I realize I'm not full of evil, buzzing butt plug anymore. Apparently my Dom managed to deal with more than the release switch. "And here?"

I want to cuddle up tighter into his chest, but I literally cannot move. "I'm fine. Utterly fantastic, actually." I haven't felt this baked after a scene in a really long time, and he deserves all the credit for that. Credit I'm just beginning to register in my own mind, because this sizzling-hot fuck says exactly the same thing the cuffs said earlier, but in a way so different I can't believe they came from the same person.

The man who touches my hair like it's spun glass and holds me tenderly and insists on my soft orgasms instead of my hard ones—this is what he picked for our first time. Up against the wall of a bar with our people right around the corner. Which would be entirely wrong for almost everyone in the universe, and so right for me. He nailed it. He got it exactly right, and that means he's nailed me, and that has nothing to do with where his cock just was and everything to do with the rest of him.

He *gets* me.

I don't know where this is going, and there's still a huge gulf between a baby Dom and an experienced, edgy switch who lives and breathes kink, but he's crossing it, one small marshmallow orgasm and mind-blasting, amazing fuck at a time.

I sigh and let myself meld even further into the man I'm sprawled on top of—and then my stomach lets out a growl loud enough to make Quint laugh around the corner.

I shake my head, or at least I try to. I don't think my neck muscles are back online yet.

Jackson rubs my belly, and I can hear his grin. "How do you feel about aftercare pizza?"

Yup. I'm nailed.

Chapter Forty

ARI

I'm starving. Three-pizzas-just-for-me levels of hungry, and the guy across from me has the audacity to look calm, sated, and amused.

He reaches into the basket of complimentary cheesy garlic breadsticks that are supposed to keep me from eating the table before our pizzas get here and hands the last one to me. I scowl at him. "Why aren't you starving?"

He shrugs.

I scowl again, but not before I demolish half the bread-stick. "Orgasms are hard work. Clearly you didn't have enough of them."

The nice older gentleman sitting at the table next to us nearly snorts his drink up his nose.

Oops. I cast Jackson an apologetic glance. My filters suck when I'm coming out of subspace.

The nice gentleman's wife reaches across the table and pats his hand—and then shoots me a conspiratorial grin that tells me I didn't do a bad thing at all. I wink back and hope I get to be her when I grow up.

She hands me their mostly full basket of breadsticks. "You

look like you could use these, dear." She gives Jackson an entirely approving look, which makes her nice gentleman chuckle and say something in a language I don't understand. It turns her ears rosy, which is stinking adorable.

Life goals.

Thirty seconds later they're walking out of the restaurant, and given the swish in her hips, I don't think their evening is over yet. Jackson is watching me, amusement all over his face.

I grin at him and chomp on another breadstick. I need to carb load my brain before it spills over on people who don't actually want a side helping of sexy vibes along with their pizza. "You've been watching me for a long time. Which I didn't know, and I'm still kind of twisted up about that, but it's given you some moves."

He dares to break off half a breadstick for himself. "The guy who taught me to play the drums was big on learning with your eyes first. I know the kink community is all about hands-on practice, and I get why, but sitting back for a while gave me a chance to learn in general and about you specifically." He makes a wry face. "Sorry if it feels creepy. I definitely didn't intend that."

Shit. "Not creepy. I'm twisted up because I didn't notice and I have a bit of a rep for eyes in the back of my head." I chomp the head off my next cheesy garlic victim. "Quint's a hands-on guy, but talk to Milo sometime. He watches better than any Dom I know, except for maybe Harlan. The two of them? They can figure out a sub before they ever touch her."

He makes a face. "It will take a really long time to get anywhere near as good as they are."

I laugh. "Duh."

I take a deep breath, because the glorious pizza-dough high is finally rescuing my crashing sub high and I'm starting to think in complete sentences. "Tell me why you picked the end of Quint's bar for our first time."

He goes totally still, but he's not sweating or apologizing or making faces. He's watching me. Those are Dom eyes.

I shake my head. "Sorry. Please tell me why, Sir."

His lips quirk. "Because it felt right. Because you'd earned it. Because you kept touching your cuffs and I wanted inside you badly enough to get off my stool and do something about it."

I tip my eyes down, which is as close as I get to submission in a vanilla public place, and smile. "Nice answer, sexy man."

He reaches forward and takes my hand, but it has all the command of fingers under my chin. "What aren't you saying?"

Dammit, the last thing I want to do is throw up all over his nice answer, but I promised him I was done hiding. I hope he can see the apology in my eyes. "I guess I'm wondering if that was mostly about meeting my needs or yours. I'm still not sure. It sounds like it was a pretty spontaneous choice, and that's okay. Your needs matter too."

He looks at me for a long time. "You're so brave everyone just expects it from you, don't they?"

Whoa. I blink, not sure where he's headed.

He shakes his head a little. "I don't ever want to be one of them. Thank you. For finding what's bothering you, and for saying it."

I'm not the only one with a rod of brave up my spine. I nod, my throat tight with the agony and the pleasure of being seen.

He takes a couple of deep breaths and lets them out. "The choice of *when* to do that scene was made in the moment and my needs were absolutely a driver. But *what* we did?" He looks a little sheepish, but his eyes don't leave mine. "I've been running scenes in my head for weeks. Ones I hoped you would like, that would let you know that I see you and I've noticed what you like and don't like and maybe even figured out a little of what you need."

It wasn't a happy accident. I take a moment to let that land and then the place inside me that's been terribly afraid to hope yanks apart the bars of the cage and roars out. "You picked it for me. It was about me."

His brow furrows. "Of course it was. And I don't think I goofed. You seemed to like what we did pretty well."

I am totally sucking at this. I grab both his hands, because somehow we're in a freaking pizzeria and I can't just crawl naked into his lap to ease the doubts that I've created with my ham-handed words. "I loved it, Jackson. I adored it. It was an entirely perfect fit with the complicated person I am who wants to be soft and loud and private and a total exhibitionist, sometimes all at the same time."

He chuckles, really quietly. "You nailed quite a few of those."

My brat beams at him. "I'm pretty sure I'm the one who got nailed."

A server walking by us nearly drops a pizza on Jackson's head. I wince. I'm a total bull in a china shop tonight.

Jackson looks up and gingerly presses upward on the perilously tilting tray.

I shake my head as tray and server and pizza all find their balance. The man totally knows just where and how hard to push.

Chapter Forty-One

JACKSON

She's still wearing my cuffs. In Seattle, nobody will ask questions, but still. It means something, or at least that's what the happy beat inside my ribs wants me to believe.

I'm not a possessive guy. I know that's why some subs walk around in cuffs and collars, but this isn't about marking my territory. It's something far more innocent than that. A visual, tangible celebration of the delight that she's chosen to be my sunbeam for a while.

I wait until the server walks away with the pizza that nearly landed in my lap and get my eyes back on the woman across from me, because she's saying really big things and she needs to know that I've heard all of them. "I think I'm a pretty simple Dom, beautiful. I'm just doing what I learned in Quint's classes. Pay attention, meet your sub's needs, fix it when you screw up."

She nods slowly. "That's what the best Doms do. It's not as simple as it looks."

She would know. "What happens when most people play with you?" I've watched, but I suddenly feel like I've missed something important.

She chews meditatively. "It depends. Lots of the time I'm training, and then I'm holding the scene along with the Dom."

I nod. "You do that sometimes with me."

I get a seriously arched eyebrow for that. "I do not. You told me not to."

I reach for her hands. Everything about her is sharper right now. I like that she's letting me see. "That wasn't an insult. You're not doing it for whole scenes, but there are moments. Like when I take both my hands off the wall and you brace yourself on your forearms so that we don't face plant. Small adjustments that I haven't learned to be on top of yet."

She snickers. "Sexy man, no Dom on Earth is on top of all of that. All experienced subs make those kinds of adjustments."

That eases something I didn't know was tight. "Maybe not quite as many as you're making for me."

She shrugs. "I don't count them. What matters is whether those adjustments are pulling me into scene-holding space, or whether they're just automatic because I've been tied to walls before and ended up with a squished nose."

She's watching me carefully as she says the last part. More carefully than seems necessary. I frown. "What?"

She shakes her head and squeezes my fingers. "Most baby Doms have a possessive streak a mile wide. You don't, and you've made that really clear, but I somehow keep expecting it to creep out."

Ah. Other scenes against other walls. "When I learned to play the drums, part of the teaching was to make your own. I did, and my first drums were really terrible. The next ones got better, but none of them came anywhere close to playing one of my teacher's old drums. They had decades of experience making music, and even if they had repairs or new skins, they had a voice that a new drum couldn't begin to touch." I wrap my hands around her cuffs. "You have a voice like that. Your experience is part of what makes you amazing."

She doesn't say a word. She just stares at me, her eyes shinier than they were.

I let my thumbs stroke the sensitive skin just above the cuffs. "I struggle with the idea of sharing you in the here and now. I think I'm still pretty vanilla on that part. But I get that the kinky world would be a lot smaller without you in it and free to be who you are."

She smiles and shakes her head slowly. "They'll live. Don't stop asking for what you need, Jackson."

I shrug and move back as the server drops three piping-hot pizzas on our table. I want to tell her I already have, but I can see that her attention has just been hijacked by the drool-worthy platters in front of her. I'm smart enough not to fight with a pizza for attention. I move slices to plates, two for us to eat and two more queued up to cool.

She lifts up her first piece and takes a tiny nibble off the end, humming happily.

I take a bite of cheese so hot it requires the burnt-tongue-sucking-air dance, but I don't let that chase away the thing I want to say next. "How am I doing on escaping your baby Dom box?"

She closes her eyes over her slice of pizza. "You know about that, do you?"

I nod. "You have good reasons."

She takes a bigger bite and does the same dance I just did. "Some of my friends think I've used those reasons to build walls I don't need."

There are more people holding a container for us than I ever would have imagined. "I know there are still big question marks about whether I can be who you need. I figure it's okay to enjoy what happened today and to celebrate it and to follow it up with some really good pizza. It doesn't mean all the doubts need to be gone. I want you to know that."

She smiles. "And you want to know how big they still are."

I borrow one of her lines. "Duh."

She laughs, but it doesn't take her long to sober. "You get it. Thank you." She takes a deep breath and squeezes my hand with her pizza-greasy fingers. "I wish the doubts weren't there. I'm working on them."

I raise an eyebrow. "*We're* working on them."

She makes a face, but I see the gratitude that sparks in her eyes. "Yes, Sir."

I chuckle and lean in, pitching my voice a lot lower than she just did. "I had no idea you were so terrible at the whole vanilla thing."

Her ears turn as pink as the lovely couple who ran away a while ago to have elder sex. "I'm sorry. I'm usually a lot better at it, but not when my brain has been recently scrambled. Public aftercare might need to be a hard limit."

Not a chance. "Ari, this is Seattle. I'm pretty sure you could stand up and announce that I spank you every morning before breakfast and most people would just grin and ask how hard."

She raises an intrigued eyebrow. "Any chance of that?"

I manage not to spill the water I just picked up. "Behave. Eat your pizza. I'll consider it."

She grins at me and chomps a huge bite out of a slice as big as her head. Apparently someone in the back room knows that Ari's pizza shouldn't be divided into ladylike wedges.

Mine, on the other hand, was apparently fair game. I pick up a second slice, determined to earn my way to pizza that gets delivered in monster quarter-pie slices. And to a more solid place inside the walls of the woman across the table. But I meant what I said. None of that needs to happen tonight.

Ari makes a strange squawking sound, mouth full of pizza.

Her face morphs through a run of emotions, most of them infused with pleasure. She's not looking at me anymore, so I turn around to see what's caught her attention.

It doesn't take long to figure out. Quint is standing just inside the door with Meghan at his side—and half of Fettered is crowding in behind them.

Chapter Forty-Two

ARI

I look around at all the peeps who matter to me, and my heart swells with the kind of happiness only my kinky tribe can deliver, even though they're not really here to deliver it for me. I know what this is, even if Jackson doesn't. This is his impromptu graduation party. He made me scream and then he turned me into a sub with no bones, and either of those would have gotten him booted out of the club's baby Dom ranks with flying colors.

I grin at Jackson. "Let me guess—you mentioned to somebody that we were going for pizza."

He raises an eyebrow at Quint. "Yeah."

Damn. Quint's never the guy leading the graduations. He likes to hold on to his trainees for as long as humanly possible.

Quint flips a chair around and takes a seat next to Jackson. "If you didn't order five thousand pizzas, we should fix that."

That won't be a problem—Mia's on duty, and she's one of ours. I raise my hand, but she's already headed our way with the kind of grin on her face that says she's been filled in on why the whole club decided to take a spontaneous pizza break.

We're about to take the place over, but this late on a Tuesday night, the other customers are already emptying out and our crew just means really good tips for the staff who choose to stick around.

Damon intercepts her, which means the boss man's buying. Mia nods and walks off with Scorpio and Mattie right behind her. Between those three, they'll make sure all the vanilla people are cleared out of harm's way in a jiffy and the only people sent to take our orders can handle overhearing jokes about anal plugs. Which likely means some of the members will get conscripted, but a decent number of them have worked here at some point, including me, so it's all good.

Jackson leans back, looking a little dazed. Chloe bends down and kisses his cheek. "About time you showed her your moves, hot stuff."

Eli growls, but it's about as effective as nicely asking kittens not to pounce.

Tank sits down next to me, pulls Eva onto his lap, and gives my Dom a look of serious respect. I have a moment to get a little worried about where this is headed, but then I see Mattie's eyes over Jackson's shoulder, and she's not looking at my slightly overwhelmed Dom. Her eyes on are me. Checking in.

Good. Not everyone thinks this is a done deal. That kind of pressure we don't need. We have a damn good start, but I know all about the deep twists and turns that live inside me. He's earned the right to try to navigate them, but Mattie's eyes say that she knows the same thing I do—even with the chops he's just put on display, there's walking left to do.

I swallow hard because I need to hold on to my brave long enough to ask him to do it—and all I really want to do right now is go plop myself in his lap and hold on for the rest of forever.

Eva's fingers wrap around mine, wordlessly saying what Mattie's eyes just did. And more. I can feel how darn happy she is for me. It's flowing out of her like an electric current.

Tank's hand strokes her hair, and for the first time in a long time, that kind of simple affection doesn't send a twinge through my ribs. She leans in and kisses my cheek. "He's a really good guy. I approve."

I snicker, because what she really means is that Jackson just landed at the top of her list of Doms to prank. "Be gentle with him. He's still learning the ropes."

Tank snorts. "Like that will stop her."

We all know it does. She's been as gentle with Tank as I've ever seen her. And as bratty, but those things kind of need to travel together. Balance.

I feel a hand seeking my thigh under the table. The migratory forces of a few dozen people joining us have pushed Jackson's chair tight against mine. I nestle into his side, enjoying the simple happiness of having someone to cuddle.

This kind of someone. I've never lacked for people to hold me when I need it, but it's different when the same person can hold you in a scene and also wake up after a mostly naked nap on his floor and laugh at your bed head.

He's not wrong that I still have doubts, and I know I owe it to both of us not to bury them. But right now, snuggled into his side with what's left of the only slice of my pizza that hasn't been stolen yet, I'm not feeling the parts that still wobble. I'm feeling the amazing amount of steady and solid that has somehow crept in. It's not that I didn't notice the trickles, but I haven't held still before now and let myself feel what they've become.

This is the kind of steady that nourishes all the dry, cracked places—the scared and doubting ones and the waiting ones and the lonely ones.

I take a bite of greasy pizza and smile.
I want so much more of this.

Chapter Forty-Three

JACKSON

She's being really quiet, but it doesn't matter. The people of Fettered are more than capable of filling a pizzeria with chatter. Most of it's even appropriate for the few vanilla people left at scattered tables, finishing their late dinners and wondering who or what the heck just invaded.

A couple of them wander over with beers, and whoever's doing informal duty on the edges deals with them. Mia is making her way through the throngs with an impressive stack of pizza platters. I didn't see anyone take orders, so presumably they're just feeding us an assortment of whatever the guys in the back have left. It won't matter with this crowd.

Scorpio starts unloading Mia's arms from the top and silver trays pass hand over hand, with a lot of funny commentary and stolen slices as they travel. Clearly they're less hot than the ones delivered to our table, which is good planning on someone's part.

"That's probably all the call-in orders that didn't get picked up." Ari finally speaks from her spot cuddled in tight to my side.

I raise an eyebrow. "That happens?"

She nods. "Usually the staff take them home, but they all just landed in a bonanza of tips, so this will keep people from eating the table legs until round two shows up."

I picked the pizza place, but clearly she's no stranger here. "Let me guess. You used to throw pizza dough around in the kitchen."

"No." Mia rolls her eyes and drops a platter in front of us. "She stuck the first couple to the ceiling and Gloria banned her from touching the dough or the pizza paddles ever again." She winks at Ari. "She has no idea she lost the skills of the best woman with a paddle in all of Seattle."

It finally registers that I've seen Mia before. At the club. In latex. Not often, and if I recall right, she has a tiny spitfire of a partner, but it's definitely her, minus the flaming-red hair, stilettos, and evil looks.

She pats me on the head. "Hi, cutie. Thanks for being exactly what my girl here needs."

Harlan growls at her and steals the last tray in her arms. "Stop treating the Doms like puppies."

She ruffles his hair instead. "I can't help it. You're all so darn cute."

Scorpio snorts and ducks under Mia and into Harlan's lap. "Poking sticks at the bears again, Mistress Mia?"

Mia grins. "You'd know something about that, wouldn't you?"

This is not the pizzeria I thought I walked into tonight, but given that it's the closest one to the club, I don't know why I'm surprised.

Scorpio makes a valiant attempt to look innocent, which sends most of the people who can see her into giggling fits. "I have no idea what you're talking about."

"Whatever." Mia leans down. "Have you given any thought

to coming to our next Domme night? You'd make a fabulous switch."

From the look on Harlan's face, this is news to him.

Scorpio rolls her eyes and leans into her guy. "I have a band to boss around. And I like the cocks I play with to still have skin on them."

I wince, along with every other guy in earshot.

Mia just chuckles and winks. "Let me know if you change your mind. Or tell Ari. She's gentler than I am."

I sense the cold wind blowing through Ari before I feel it in her body. There's not much to feel. A small catch in her breath. A tiny stiffening, barely the length of a heartbeat before she releases it. But it's there.

There, and she's trying to hide it.

I can also see the quick glances our way. The polite avoidance as people wait to see if I noticed. If I'm going to do anything about it.

I could, but if the last decade of my life has taught me anything, it's about the importance of rhythm. Of the spaces between the beats. We've had a big day, and nothing in me wants to add to it. I'm not done climbing the mountain of Ari yet and we both know that, but I don't need to do the rest of it tonight.

We have time, and she's got a week of really slow, quiet orgasms coming to her before we embark on anything else.

But I can do something about the belief, crackling in this pizzeria like a live wire, that I somehow haven't noticed that Ari's a switch. I pull her in a little closer and kiss the top of her head. "For the record, I kind of like my cock with skin on it too. In case that matters."

This time, the wind that blows through her is hot and jerky and she tries to hide that too. Not that it exists, but how big it is. How necessary it is to who she is. How my words matter somewhere deep—and how much they surprise her.

I do my job and stand in the hot wind right beside her, looking straight at the mountain of one of her doubts. I don't try to tear it down. Words won't do that, and I'm well aware I'm not ready. I have no idea what to do with this part of who she is, but I know it's on the table. I've always known, and no matter what else I get wrong, and I will, I will never ask her to be less than who she is.

I try to say all that with my silence, because pizzerias and tribal gatherings are for eating, not for tearing hard things out of the soil and peering at their roots.

All I want her to know right now is that I'm steady and I see.

Chapter Forty-Four

ARI

A week. A whole freaking week.

I glare at the hook on the end of Quint's bar as I walk by it. Scene of the crime, and my Dom is totally making me pay for all the noise I made when he strung me up and had his way with me. A whole week of gooey soft orgasms, and I have no idea when he's going to bust me out of marshmallow prison.

I grin and pour myself a pink virgin margarita. Subs are honor-bound to complain, and I will, but all Jackson has done in the last week is cement my pussy's love affair with his fingers. And with the slapper. And, one very inventive night, with his drumsticks. The man is frightfully good with percussion instruments, even if he's sticking to the kind I generally think of as the kiddie bench.

Quint wasn't wrong about all this stuff being different when your heart is involved.

Which is going to make today tricky. I have a demo to do, which is something I do several times a week and they never make me blink—but this one seems custom designed to see if Jackson will. It isn't intentional. It's been on the schedule for two months, and it's a classic Ari thing to be doing, but the timing still feels loaded.

I didn't help any by not mentioning it when I left his bed for work this morning. A conscious choice, and not the one I would usually make, but this doesn't belong in marshmallow land and he's not a Dom who needs to be babied. At least I hope those were my reasons. It's possible it was just good, old-fashioned avoidance.

I reach up and touch the hook and let my eyes drift to the cuffs I wear more often than not these days. It pleases him, but that's only a nice side effect. They please me, in some soft, gooey, deep-inside place I knew I had but didn't know he could touch. Not like this, anyhow. Not while I still have doubts.

It's wondrous that he can—and it's scary as fuck.

I head back to the club's small change room, running my fingers over the weaving of the cuffs as I walk. They need to come off today, which seems more potent and symbolic than I want it to be. I lean my forehead against the cool steel of my locker. This is part of me too. I can't put a lid on it just because it might make my Dom uncomfortable. He said he's watched me before, and when it came up at the pizzeria, he didn't run.

I shake my head. I should have said something this morning. I can feel it as an act of avoidance now, and that tells me things I don't want to know about the state of my insides. How Jackson feels about this part of me matters, maybe too much. The consequences of the gooey parts of us moving too fast for the rest to keep up.

I huff out a breath and reach into my locker for my favorite pair of latex pants. I can't think about this now. Mistress A has an appointment to keep.

Chapter Forty-Five

JACKSON

There aren't a whole lot of things that can disrupt my drumming. Watching my sub walk into the lounge in shiny black leather from breasts to toes is absolutely one of them.

She doesn't look like a sub tonight. A shiny black corset shows off a lot of skin and even more of the sensual power she's put on. Skintight pants and boots that look like they stepped out of a steampunk novel. No stilettos for Ari. She doesn't need them. Dominance isn't a height thing, it's a mindset, and nobody with a brain would doubt this woman has it.

She turns for another pitcher of whatever she's pouring, and I can make out the lariat attached to the chain belt riding her hips. Probably a crop on the other side, but black on black on shadow means I'm mostly getting impressions, not details.

Impressions are enough. She's stunning, golden confidence encased in black. I'm just not sure she's mine, and that would be what's messing up my drum beats.

I can feel the eyes of the rest of the band on me. I don't bother checking, because I know what I would see. Scorpio, daring me to step up and ready to hold my drumsticks while I do it. Eli with the steady look of a guy who's walked his own tunnel of risks and come out the other side. He likely under-stands better than most. Chloe's not a Domme, but she can impersonate one really well. Quint's the only one I can't be sure of. He's my trainer, and he's had my back every damn step of this walk so far, even the ones where he maybe thinks I'm fucking up. But Ari's his little sister, and she's in here for one reason and one reason only, and it's not so that she can pour a bunch of drinks.

She only looks at me once. A quick glance, and it's not loaded at all. Just a club Domme going about her business.

The loaded part is up to me.

I take my first real breath as she pushes back through the swinging doors into the dungeon. Scenes happen in there. I've watched her in action, but not since I got permission to touch her, and every inch of this is hitting me differently now that I have.

I hit a roll on my drum and realize I'm the only person left playing. I stop, not sure whether the song halted or whether I just kept going past its end, but either way, there are three people waiting for me to do something other than keep the beat.

I take another solid breath and meet Quint's eyes. He's got his poker face on, which doesn't tell me anything useful. I shrug a shoulder in the direction Ari just headed. "Are the Dommes meeting tonight?"

His shoulders relax fractionally. "Yeah. There are a few guys in there too. Anyone with male subs. She's doing a CBT demo."

I wince and my cock winces harder.

Scorpio raises a questioning eyebrow.

"Cock ball torture," says Eli quietly.

Scorpio snickers. "Maybe I should go watch."

Maybe I should too. I freeze in a rare moment of indecision, half my body still on the stool, half headed into the dungeon.

Quint just watches me, and he isn't wearing his poker face anymore. There's a dare in his eyes, but I'm not sure what it is.

It doesn't matter. This is on me and on what I think my sub needs, even when she's not being my sub. I lay down my sticks and get my ass all the way off my stool. "I'll be back in a while."

I can feel all of their eyes on me as I cross the lounge and push through the door.

Then I'm all out of time to worry about what's behind me. I'm way too busy staring at what's in front of me. Four tables laid out in a rough square, and four guys strapped down in various states of mostly naked. I don't recognize any of them, but I can see enough shakes and questions to guess that they're all fairly new—or the tops at their sides are. Amelia is roaming between tables, as are a couple of the other experienced Dommes. Ari's at the side of a gorgeous six-foot-tall redhead, murmuring quiet instructions.

I look down at the device the redhead is trying to put on her sub and shiver.

The redhead glares at her sub. "This would be a lot easier if you didn't have an erection."

He grins up at her, totally unrepentant. "Sorry, Mistress, but you're touching me, and that's really hot."

Ari gives him a dirty look. "Quit fucking with her, Sean."

The redhead raises an eyebrow. "Messing with me, is he?" The hold she takes on his balls looks less than friendly. "I thought we talked about that. No taking advantage of my inexperience or I'll sit you in a corner while I practice on someone else."

Sean looks like he's going to pout and then thinks better of it. "Sorry, Mistress." This time he mostly sounds like he means it.

Ari hasn't seen me yet, but Amelia has—and if I thought Quint's eyes held a dare, they've got nothing on the fierce look she pins on me. I meet her gaze as calmly as I can, given how many tortured cocks are currently in my line of sight.

She walks over to me. "Normally we don't allow audience members who aren't part of the group, but I'll make an exception in your case if you can stop wincing."

I make a face, but my eyes are mostly on my sub. "Sorry."

She chuckles. "I remember the first time I watched a scene with nipple clamps. I left that night wondering why any woman would ever want to be a submissive."

That's part of what's going on inside me, but not all. I'm far more interested in the walls of glass that seem to be up around my sub. There's no connection. No energy flowing between us. I study the pair she's trying to help. Sean looks less aroused now, but judging from the redhead's level of frustration, that isn't solving the problem.

She jams the device into Ari's hands. "Show me. Please."

For the first time, Ari's eyes rise up to meet mine. "I can't, I'm sorry. No hands-on for me tonight."

The redhead's eyes widen. "Why? That's how we learn best."

Ari looks at her and nods. "I know, and my flogger demo later will be live. But I'm exploring a relationship with someone right now. We talked about boundaries during these demos, but I'm realizing we didn't do it in enough detail." She glances at me, and for the first time, there's warmth in her eyes, and humor, and apology. "Which is a rookie error on my part, but until I know what he thinks about my hands on someone else's cock, I'm going to stick to walking you through this with my words."

It's a fluid, easy answer, one spoken by someone who has navigated this world for years and done it with fearless integrity. Which gets my feet moving before she's done speaking, even though my cock is trying to run screaming the other way. "He's thinking that you maybe need a volunteer with a cock you're welcome to touch."

Chapter Forty-Six

ARI

Everyone is staring at him. Me too, but I'm not the one who's most surprised.

Tracey, who is closest to him and new to this and still convinced she needs to use anger to project power, looks him up and down, disdain on her face. "You're not a sub."

Jackson keeps his eyes on me. "No, I'm not."

This man. He knows how to throw us off the deep end with just his words, but I'm not going to let him go swimming alone. I pull my shit as back together as I can get it in a breath. "Then why are you volunteering?" There are a lot of answers to that question that will have me stopping this scene before it goes any further, but I can see his eyes. I don't think he's going to give me one of them.

He smiles at me. "Because I'm exploring a relationship with someone right now and we haven't explored this."

Right answer. Really right answer. But I drop both of us on our heads if I say that, along with most of the people watching us—although I may end up doing that anyway. I'm about to break one of the most basic rules of kink, and there are only a handful of people in here who will even begin to understand why.

Amelia is watching me and she's one of them. She's also the long-time queen of these meetings, and she hasn't put a stop to this yet. Which means she thinks there's value in people getting to watch this, even if it could turn into an absolute clusterfuck.

I keep my eyes on the man who will decide that. "I don't tie up Doms."

He lifts his shoulders a little. "I'm not a Dom right now. I'm just a guy." He looks at the device in my hands and I see his nerves, but he doesn't say anything.

Amelia steps forward, into a line where I can see her eyes without taking them off Jackson. "It's rare to have a chance to see a demo with a brand-new sub. Perhaps you might change your focus for tonight, Mistress A."

She's not leading me, exactly, but she's trying to help. Letting me off the hook of what I was supposed to do and making that clear for everyone. Clearing the way for me to do what I need to do and what Jackson needs me to do, because this is about way more than him volunteering to get his cock stuffed in a cage.

I stretch my spine, long and tall and supple, breathing into all of who I am when I'm Mistress A. And then I wink at my guy, because he needs to know that some parts of me don't change. "Your safewords are yellow and red, same as usual. What are your limits for tonight?"

I can hear the quiet huffs of air around me. I'm hooking up the safety lines to a scene and they know it. They're not the only ones. The door behind Jackson has slid open, and his band is lining up behind him, shoulder to shoulder. Holding us, but I'm not sure he'll see it that way.

He watches me for a long moment. "The same ones Quint uses for beginner trainees."

Smart. And brave. That leaves a lot of territory, and he knows I'm capable of taking him into any of it. I line up the things I most need to confirm, because Dommes tend to work a little differently than the topping he's used to thinking through. "So public nudity, sexual touch, orgasm, light to moderate impact play."

He nods. I haven't shaken him yet.

I need to. "Humiliation?"

His eyebrows shoot up, and I see his answer long before he finds polite words to tell me. He shakes his head. "No. Hard limit."

I smile. "Why?"

His smile back is wry. "Because that doesn't feel like respect to me, and I'm getting that in a totally different way than I ever did in Dom shoes."

Amelia chuckles behind me. "He'll do."

He looks at her, which is a total breach of protocol, but I don't much care. "I don't mean any judgment to people who use it. I know you do, Mistress Amelia, and I know your subs feel like they're better people after you're done with them."

Dead silence—and a whole lot of interested, assessing looks.

I growl. *Mine.*

Jackson's eyes fly to my face.

I flick my chin at the line of hard-asses over his shoulder. "Any restrictions on who watches?"

He turns around slowly. Scorpio smirks at him. The other two just glower. Jackson might have stepped out of his Dom shoes for a while, but Quint and Eli are clearly committing to holding the territory until he gets back. Just in case anyone tries a sneak invasion.

Jackson turns back around and faces me. He takes a breath, and the nerves are sharper now. "I'm fine with that."

A gift. One that he's clearly, quietly offering me because he knows I need this part of who I am to be seen. By him and by them and by everyone. A gift that comes with weight, because this isn't just about me. It's about us, and I'm the top in this scene and the pressure of that is a sudden fire in my belly.

He needs me not to fuck this up. He needs me to unwrap my gift and appreciate every bit of him, even if he's about to struggle like hell.

The fire fuses my backbone into Domme steel. I let him see it in my eyes. "Strip, gorgeous. Everything off."

Chapter Forty-Seven

JACKSON

Naked is easy. I tell myself that as I slide the shirt over my head.

There's an appreciative murmur from my left, one Ari doesn't even seem to notice. Fine. I take my cues from her. No one else matters. I ditch my boots, and this time the murmurs are more widespread and hold notes of humor.

Ari's eyes crinkle. "Nice balance, sexy man."

Okay, the whole approval thing is really weird from this end. Especially for something as simple as not falling over while I unlace my boots. I shrug and unzip my jeans, giving them and my boxers a good shove toward the floor, and then I stop moving, likely looking at least as awkward as I feel. I have no idea what the protocol is at this point. I'm pretty sure it's not to stand with my pants around my legs, but she hasn't given me any instructions, either.

She nods, and this time her approval wraps around me and brushes away some of the nerves. "Step out of your pants. Follow me."

She turns and heads toward the back wall. I can hear

clinking and clattering and hushed instructions as I ditch my pants and follow her. People freeing up their subs. Everyone coming to watch.

I'm a drummer. What I do gets better, more important, more potent, when it has an audience. I have no idea whether I care about people staring at my naked ass or not, but I do know I want them watching Ari, because what's streaming off of her right now is absolutely fucking potent and the world needs to see it.

When she reaches the wall and turns to face me, I realize what I'm seeing in the lines of her body is nothing compared to what lives in her eyes. On her face. In every molecule of what she's sending my way.

Complete control. Holding me. Holding us.

Something worried inside of me relaxes. It's okay if I mess this up, if I have no idea how to be a baby sub. She knows. She's got this and she's got us and all I have to do is try not to bumble into her way too much.

Her face is all Domme, but there's something warm in her eyes as she holds out her hands. "Give me your wrists."

It's a simple instruction until I see what she's holding.

Her cuffs. The ones I made her.

The dungeon is dead silent. Everyone knows what they are. What they mean.

Whatever just tensed inside me relaxes. I know what they mean too, and it doesn't matter which one of us is wearing them. They're still the very tangible symbol of the two of us giving what lives between us a chance. I hold out my wrists, both of them, and hope she can read the rest of my message in her careful study of my body.

Gladly, beautiful. I'm all yours.

She puts on the cuffs with fast, competent care. Then she

wraps her fingers over them and looks up at me—and there's a glint in her eyes that's my first warning. All the nerves she's been calming fire back up with a vengeance.

Mistress A is in the house.

Chapter Forty-Eight

ARI

He's amazing and he's mine and the possessive, crazy joy of that is already sending me into topspace, which is a place I go hardly ever. I need to not go there now, or I'm going to blow up the trust that just put his wrists in my hands.

He's not a sub. I know that, with everything that's in me. But he's an explorer, someone who dives deep into who he is, and he's willing to do this to learn more about himself and to let me shine. Which is a bunch of words to say that he's doing this for me and it's okay for me to let him. He's not hurting himself to do it. And I'm good enough to do this and not make him smaller.

I grin and take back that last thought. I might make some parts of him shrivel a little.

He's smart enough that wariness flashes in his eyes. I don't let it live there long. I've seen this man drum—I'm not going to have to demand his surrender. I just need to build him a good enough reason to give it. I lift one arm over his head, pleased that he lets me bear its weight. I clamp it on to a steel bar sticking straight out from the wall. Another one of Milo's inventions. Same functionality as a wall hook, but it lets me keep my sub facing out.

I can see the sheepish humor in Jackson's eyes as I lift his second arm over his head. He's recognizing the parallels, which is going to make this fun. Sadly for him, he's not getting a quickie around the side of the Quint's bar. Ari would give him that in a hot minute, but Mistress A has different priorities.

She wants to honor his gift.

I bring myself in close to his ear. He has no idea how to be a sub, and there are practicalities involved. "Let the cuffs take your weight. If you feel pain or tingling in your arms or hands or shoulders, I need to know right away."

He nods, and I can see him adjusting. Testing his weight in the cuffs.

I smile as he lets his head relax against his extended arm. Smart man. I run a finger down his cheek. Amelia would use a crop for this part, but he touches me constantly in scenes and I don't think he does it just for me. I will want an impact toy, though, and the perfect one suddenly beams into my brain. I crook a finger at Mia and send her hand signs. She can ogle Jackson's ass later. Right now I need her to go grab me a toy.

Her eyebrows slide up, but she heads off to do my bidding. Which is good, because the only sub in the room who hasn't been recently tied up is Scorpio, and she's been taking too many brat lessons from Sam for me to trust her on this particular errand.

Instructions given, I move back to Jackson, letting my eyes run up and down his body, so that he can see that I'm watching and so I can measure his reactions. Male subs are a lot easier to read in some ways, but I'm a smart enough Domme not to rely on his cock as a gauge. It gives a twitch or two as I look at it, but he's not a guy who's turned on purely by the idea of what I might do to him next. He's not afraid of it either. There are nerves, but he's letting me see them, and they're small.

I hope Tracey is paying attention. Anger isn't necessary, and neither is fear.

There's no bigger source of power in the entire world than trust.

Chapter Forty-Nine

JACKSON

She's barely touching me and I'm already feeling weirdly melted. It takes me a minute, and when I figure it out, I almost laugh. Ari has to be bribed, threatened, and tormented to head into her softness.

Apparently I'm easy.

The strange things you learn when you're naked and strung up in a dungeon. However, the message of naked and strung up is only reinforcing what rides in Ari's every breath and touch and look. I'm not in charge. She doesn't need me to be or want me to be and every time I soften, something important inside her gets a chance to grow.

I know my answer in a heartbeat.

If she wants my bones, she has them.

Her fingers trail down my chest, drawing a trail through my light curls, scraping a fingernail across my nipple. I see the glint in her eyes as she does that again, and I realize there's not a damn thing I can do if she wants to stand here for the next hour scratching at my nipples.

That's the thing that makes my cock go hard. Not the

fingernails. The realization that I'm entirely, completely at her mercy.

She glances down and back up at me, her eyebrows rising slightly.

I hope she doesn't think it's the fingernails.

She chuckles and traces a path down, detouring around my belly button and my naive, hopeful cock. She draws her fingernails up my thigh, which apparently triggers every nerve ending from there to my balls.

She does it again and I groan.

She smiles and taps her fingers on my cock, hard enough to remind me of the nasty devices in use when I first came in. I wince. I've seen Mistress A in action. She's not generally a kind-and-gentle Domme. The sounds of the crowd whisper over us, a little louder. They know it too.

She swishes her crop through the air and the noise utterly silences.

I'd grin, but I'm a little too much in awe right now. She's not just dominating me, she's got the whole dungeon submitting. I wonder how many of them know it.

Ari clears her throat just loudly enough for me to hear. Oops. Mind wandering, and even I know better than that.. I lean my head against my arm and watch her eyes. I don't know how long she's going to let me do that, but for right now, they let me see all my best reasons for doing this.

Her eyes sharpen and she reaches for me, running competent hands up my ribs to my shoulders. Not trying to arouse this time, just checking in.

I check in too, but my arms are fine. Stretchy. Limber. Like a strange extension of my belly. I'm sure parts of me will feel strangely used tomorrow, but my arms aren't at the top of my concern list. They've been driven to the point of exhaustion and lived to tell the tale more times than I can count.

Something raps sharply against my thigh. I jump and look down, but it isn't her crop that's hit me. I look back up and give her a scowl that's probably going to get me in deep trouble. "That's my drumstick."

She merely raises an eyebrow, but it says everything she needs to say.

Shit. I manage to get a grip on the rest of what I want to say, but it's hard to let go. My drumsticks are like a limb, an extension of who I am, and using them this way feels like an invasion. I promised her me. I didn't promise her my drumsticks.

It takes another ragged breath before the rest sinks in. The focus in her eyes. The hand on my chest. The fact that the drumstick hasn't so much as quivered again in her hand.

She's holding the scene together with nothing but quiet power—and she's waiting.

I have no idea for what, though. I might be a baby Dom and an even greener sub, but it's not up to me to give permission.

And then it hits me. Why she's using them. My drumsticks are a part of me—and a part of the one place where I know, absolutely, how to surrender.

She's trying to help.

Chapter Fifty

ARI

Fuck. That was a close call, and everyone in this dungeon knows it except for maybe Jackson. Until I saw the look on his face, I had no freaking idea just how much his drumsticks mean to him. Pushing edges as hard as I do sometimes means you step over them, but I wasn't trying to push, and it's only his generosity that has gotten us back on the right side of the line.

I let out a breath I hope he can't hear and tilt my head in a barely perceptible nod. We'll talk about consent later and how badly I screwed up, but his generosity deserves a reward, and I want so very badly to be the person who hands it to him. Because however badly I stumbled on the way in this particular door, he gets why I chose it now. I've seen him play his drums, and wherever it is that musicians go isn't all that far from subspace.

I keep my hand on his chest, as anchor and apology both, and run the shaft of the drumstick lightly up the side of his ribs. Then I rap it on his sternum, just to amuse us both.

His lips quirk, but other than that, he's managed to get himself back into very presentable sub demeanor. I tap the drumstick gently, straight down the line of his belly and onto the base of his very interested cock. I wrap my other hand around his cock and give a good, strong squeeze.

His breath huffs out, and he hardens more in my hand.

Today's demo was supposed to be about teaching a sub erection control, but I can't think of a single reason why I want to do that. Not with this man. There are other ways to make his pleasure entirely up to me, and I've always been a better tease than a disciplinarian.

I play with him a little, alternating fisting with fun little taps with his drumstick. It's not a bad impact toy, although it has absolutely no bend, which I need to remember when things start moving faster. His eyes are down on his cock, which I can't blame him for—it's a pretty picture. And one I'm going to take away from him soon enough.

I work until he's aroused enough that I can feel the throbbing when I wrap my fingers around his cock and his breath is starting to come fast and shallow. Then I trace the drumstick up his body, moving slowly. Pulling his attention to a single focus point. He's so visual, and I could work with that, but I'm curious about what lies underneath.

The drumstick glides, outlining his collarbone, up the side of his neck, stopping by his temple. "Close your eyes, gorgeous."

He stares at me, and it's one of those looks where I know he hasn't quite processed the words yet. When he does, his eyes glide easily closed.

I watch a few seconds longer, but he's solid. A man who knows how to be in the dark. "I will permit you a choice. You can keep your eyes closed for me, or I can use a blindfold."

He's still a moment, and then he nods. "I'll keep them closed. Thank you."

I wait a moment, but he doesn't add a title. Which is when

I know just how closely he's watched me all these months. Most subs use a title, and it's not something I correct in a casual scene—but it's not something I appreciate or seek either. This isn't Dom ego or beginner forgetfulness. He knows.

No titles, because in the end, I'm not two things, I'm one.

I let the glow of that warm my insides. He sees me, and I channel that, because it's exactly the gift I want to give him. I brush my fingertips over his face, over his closed eyelids. Then I start a slow, stately walk around him. I don't touch him at first. I want him to tune in to his other senses. The sound of my footsteps. The changes in the air currents as I move around him. The beautiful energy that connects Domme and sub when they're doing it right, and we are.

He quiets his movement, his breath, his thoughts. Even his cock softens some. Not from a lack of desire. From attention. His whole focus is on me, and in this moment, kink isn't sexual. It's two souls entirely attuned to each other.

Chapter Fifty-One

JACKSON

She's everywhere. I can hear her breathing like it's right next to my ear, but her footsteps are behind me. Something swishes through the air, and I wait for drumstick or crop to land, but nothing does. Just sounds.

She hums, and it's a sound I know. She makes it when something feels good. My cock lights up. He knows what that means. We're pleasing Ari.

My head wouldn't have understood six months ago, but I've been a Dom long enough to get it. Sometimes the pleasure isn't from doing or being done to, it's just from being. From inhaling the electric tug of power and knowing it exists because two people have agreed that it should.

I've never been on this end of the tug—but I can feel it. And I can feel how different it is for her. She chooses to be a sub, but however much fun she has along the way, surrender pushes on her. This version of Ari is light. Easy. Her footsteps aren't a march. They're what happens right before lightning dances.

I wait. If she wants to dance in a storm, I'm her guy.

I feel a change in the electricity just before the drumstick lands again, this time right between my shoulder blades. Then her fingers, brushing over my ass. The storm starts off slowly, as she keeps moving in her stately spiral around me, dropping random touches and blows, some hard enough to sting, some so ephemeral I barely feel them.

A sharp crack on my ass, and I hear the murmured approval in the room. I let it wash over me. I never expected to be on this end of a spanking, but I can deal.

Except that's not where Mistress A is taking this. She's still moving, and the touches are getting more intimate. A drumstick rolling up my inner thighs. A fingernail across my nipple. A kiss on my ribs. A rapid series of taps on the underside of my cock, which somehow doesn't discourage him any. A sound I don't recognize and then a cool slide of lube down my ass crack.

She doesn't stay with any of them long enough for me to do more than react, and eventually I stop doing that too. I stop moving. Stop trying to guess where she's coming in next. Stop trying to find the beat in a dance that doesn't have one. I just wait.

A soft, pleased hum again, and strong fingers wrap around my cock, rewarding him with quick, well-lubed tugs. A groan leaks out of me, and the need in my belly flames.

Two more quick strokes and she's gone again.

My cock weeps. He's just beginning to figure out just how much this could suck. The rest of me can't stay focused on that thought. I'm too busy following her touch.

Her hands are landing harder now and so is the drumstick. Heating up my skin. Reminding me of nights around an African fire. It's primal and it's raw and all the veneers of Jackson who functions in the day-to-day of modern, multi-tasking Seattle are cracking off and falling away under the beat of her hands.

She lands a stinging swat to the side of my cock a fraction off-beat, and the hitch in the rhythm hurts far more than the hot prickles on my skin. It's not an accident. She knows exactly how much rhythm matters to me and she's messing with it with deliberate, impressive precision. Something so very damn close—but not quite.

Another swat, this time straight up under my balls, and another hitch in the beat.

I can hear the frustration in my groan. She's got an evil sense of timing. If she ever lets me out of these cuffs, she's getting a hand-drumming lesson. She'll be wicked good at it.

I don't know if my groan is the trigger, but she lets loose a wild storm of blows and taps on my back, my ass, my hamstrings. If I didn't know her integrity, I'd swear she had help. It feels like a lot more than two hands working me over, pushing me into the center of the storm, raining their fury down on my wide-awake skin.

My cock leaps every time she moves, breaths, hums, beats. Begging to be hit by lightning.

Chapter Fifty-Two

ARI

I planned this as warm-up. A little sensory play to get him focused on me before we headed in to the real deal. Except my guy surprised me, and he's made this real. The signs are all there. Absolute focus, utter presence, every inch of him ready to surrender on my command.

He's making this easy.

As someone who's stood on the edge of that precipice more times than I can count and struggled to go over every damn time, I'm in awe. He's not struggling, he's not demanding that I finish this, he's not resisting anything other than the occasional mess I make of what he considers to be an acceptable beat.

His Dom surrendered the moment he volunteered. The man has joined him. All that's left resisting is the drummer, and I don't need his submission.

I even up the beat and stop tormenting him. It's time to finish this.

I move in front of him. There are a lot of directions I could take this and it's not ego to say I can make all of them work, but this isn't about my Domme skills or even about his submission anymore.

It's come full circle. This is about us.

I lean in and put my hands on his chest. "Open your eyes, Jackson." I use his name—I'm pretty sure it's going to take that much to pull him out of where he's gone.

His eyes slide open, and the haze in them is beautiful.

I move one hand up to his cheek and wrap the other around his cock.

His gaze sharpens, but he doesn't move. This isn't the obedience of someone who craves submission. It's a choice. A gift. He's going to let me take this right to the end.

A couple of twisting strokes to his cock and he's right there, ready and entirely willing and aware and needy as fuck. I smile and give him a look he should recognize. Mistress A and my brat are two sides of a very skinny coin.

I can see the answer in his eyes. He knows I could hold him here. He's willing.

Which is when I feel it flip inside me. The switch that lives inside all of us who play both ends of the power game. I let it happen, even though by rights it should be scene suicide. His eyes and my insides say we can do this. That we need to do this.

Slowly, I sink down into a crouch, never taking my eyes off his. I kneel down at his feet and open my hands, palms in front of his cock, ready to catch. And smile. "Now, sexy man. Come for me now."

Chapter Fifty-Three

JACKSON

She's not even touching me.

That's all I have time to think before the lightning of release shoots down my spine and rolls thunder out my balls. I'm tied to the ceiling and coming all over Ari's outstretched hands and it's the most surreal moment of my life—and one of the most real. She might be down on her knees in front of me, but her eyes are still holding us with that amazing power of hers that's not just about dominance but something absolutely essential to the core of who she is.

She climbs to her feet as my body shakes with the storm that isn't yet entirely done and leans her head into my shoulder. I ache to hold her, but the ceiling somehow still has possession of my arms. I lay my head down on the top of hers and breathe. Just breathe. We're almost done with the thunder and lightning, but I know what comes after that.

The glorious smell of the earth just after it rains.

I listen to the ragged sounds of my breath as she wipes us both down with a warm, wet towel that materialized from somewhere, and feel into the newness. Into what we've just become in her hands, in her care, in her consummate skill.

I've been railing against the label of baby Dom. Now I get it. If she's my standard, I might be wearing that label for the rest of my life.

I feel movement behind me, and I resist. This is our space. I'm not ready for anyone else.

"Ssh." She wraps her arms around my waist and holds on. "It's Quint. He's just going to unhook your arms."

It's quick. Milo's magnets release in an instant, and I've never really understood before just how profoundly awesome that is. Two strong hands guide my arms down to my sides, and then nobody is in our bubble anymore. I try to flop my spaghetti limbs in a way that might wrap around Ari, and fail utterly.

She chuckles and kisses my chest. "Can you walk? There's a couch in the corner just behind you."

I'm not sure I can walk, but the alternative is slumping into a puddle where I stand, so I try. My arms feel strange and long, like my knuckles should be dragging on the ground. Ari doesn't let go of my waist as we shuffle over to a couch that someone's thoughtfully draped with one of the cozy aftercare blankets Fettered stocks by the crate. My bare ass is grateful. If I stick to the leather, I might never get back up.

Ari fusses for a bit, getting me comfortable, fetching a stool for my long legs that don't fit on the couch, tucking a pillow behind my head. I let her. My gorilla arms haven't figured out how to function yet, and there's something going on with her that I don't quite understand. I can't see it—she looks like a veteran Domme taking care of her sub. But I can feel it.

She sits on the couch beside me and touches my cheek. "Is it okay if I straddle your legs?"

I nod. My words haven't really figured out how to work yet either.

She lifts and settles in a way that I hadn't imagined latex pants could stretch and cuddles into my chest. She doesn't stay, though. She sits right back up, opens a bottle of arnica gel, and starts massaging one of my arms. It's not gentle—a few brisk rubs up and down and then her thumbs poke right into the gorilla and tell him to get lost.

I squirm a little, because I checked my Dom card at the door tonight. "Scene's over, beautiful. You can stop torturing me now."

She chuckles. "This is help, I promise. Trust someone who's been tied to a lot of hooks."

I wince again. "I didn't rub your arms enough, did I?"

She shakes her head and kisses my cheek. "You did fine. I know how to work with the restraints. You don't, although you're going to be a lot less sore than most because you didn't fight them."

The words sound like standard, friendly, analytical Ari, but I hear something else in them. Something that makes me squirm and expand all at the same time.

Pride.

I clear my throat and wait for her to look at me. "You were amazing." Those are weak words for what I mean to say, but the gorilla has only moved far enough to take a seat on my brain.

She smiles at me and closes her eyes for a moment, just breathing. When she opens them again, my soft Ari is back. She cups my face and kisses me very gently. "Thank you."

Chapter Fifty-Four

ARI

I hear the rumble beside us before I see the bottle of electrolyte drink. The list of people who would dare to interrupt me in aftercare is really short, and this one has hairy knuckles.

Quint puts a hand on my shoulder and hands me a bottle too. "He's crashing and you're close. Don't be idiots."

I wince and Jackson growls.

I stare at him, because nobody growls at Quint, especially when they're naked and very recently tied up.

Quint just chuckles, unscrews the lid on my bottle, and walks away.

Jackson picks up the arm I was almost done rubbing down and pulls me in closer to his chest. "I'm fine, and nobody gets to give you shit for what just happened between us."

I take a long swig of electrolytes. "Even when he's right?"

"Yes." Jackson tips back his bottle and drinks long and deep. Then he looks at me. "Have we reached the part of this yet where you get to curl up in my lap and I can just hold you for a while?"

My Dom is back. "I was thinking of something more along the lines of your head in my lap so that I can play with your curls." And so that he can get some blood back in his head, but I don't say that part.

He smiles into my hair. "That sounds nice. Save it for later? I'll put on a fire."

A pillow nest in front of his fireplace is one of my favorite places and he knows it. I tuck in a little closer. Clearly he can get his blood to wherever he needs it to be. "Do you want your pants?"

I can hear his eyebrows going up. And his honest confusion. "Why?"

Some day I'm going to stop assuming this man is like any other Dom I know. "Because people are probably going to come over soon and want to talk to us, and I thought you might want to be less naked."

He snorts. "Are these the same people who just saw you turn me into a very naked human drum?"

That's a really sweet description of a surprisingly intense scene—and he's not wrong. About becoming my drum or about how much anyone else is going to care what he's wearing. "Yes. Those people."

He shakes off the rest of my half-assed massage and wraps both arms around me. "They need to stay away for a while. I'm not done sinking into what just happened yet."

That makes two of us. "You surrender better than I do."

I feel the smile into my hair. "Just more easily. We get to the same place."

We do, and that matters too. I go hard into that particular dark night, but when I get there, I go deep. He sailed in light as a feather, but it didn't dampen the depth of his journey any.

He strokes my hair, which melts all my bones. "How often do you need to do that?"

I listen, but there's no loading behind his words. No answer he needs. Just honest curiosity. I push myself back up, because

I need to see his eyes for this. "I don't know. I've never really been here."

It takes him a moment. "In a relationship with someone willing to do both parts with you?"

More than one kind of new. "I haven't even been in very many relationships, really. And they've all been with Doms." I frown, because I need to be careful with my words, but I also need to tell the truth. "You're not a switch."

He grins and shifts my ass in closer to his cock. "Are you sure about that, Mistress Bossypants?"

I snort. "I dare you to call Amelia that."

He rolls his eyes. "No thank you. I saw that thing she was holding, and I'm very sure she knows how to use it."

He even gives me this—the chance to use levity to breathe space into who we are. To make enough room for all the things I want to pull into the light. "Do you think you're a switch?"

His head shake is fast and sure, his grimace slower. "My first answer's no, but that's probably a dumb thing to say after what just happened."

This is the truth I need him to hear. "Not dumb at all." I trace my fingers through the hair on his chest. "Switches are people who *need* to play with both sides of power exchange. I don't think you do."

He's listening, quiet and thoughtful and not at all ready to agree. "Maybe switches are people who can grow from playing both sides."

Smart, insightful, interesting man. I sigh and lean back in. "I have this pet theory that almost everyone, kinky or not, switch or not, could benefit from stepping into both roles at least a few times. There are things you learn when you're trussed up or holding a paddle in your hand that you just can't learn any other way."

His chest rumbles as he laughs. "I bet."

I snort. His cock is waking up underneath me, which probably means someone needs to give him paddle lessons. I will gladly offer my ass to the cause. "But being capable of learning from an experience doesn't mean you need it. You figured out how to make tonight work for you and you're digging in to what it gave you, but you did it for me."

His hands wrap around my shoulders and he sits me back up, firmness in his eyes. "For you, and for us. We're better if you have a chance to go there. It lights you up, and I don't ever want to get in the way of that." He grins. "I might even enjoy some of it."

Chapter Fifty-Five

JACKSON

I'm high. I know it and I don't care, and I don't think it's scene leftovers that are doing it. It's the fumes of what's happening between us right now. She's flustered and beautiful and I love that she's never done this before. I tuck her hair behind her ears, because keeping her flustered and beautiful feels like an awesome goal in life. "So what do you think—fifty-fifty on who's wearing the cuffs?"

She laughs and pulls my wrist up to her face, planting a kiss on the weaving that I never, ever imagined was going to become something this pivotal in my life.

I run my hands down to her hips. We're laughing, but this is also deadly serious. "What do you think you need, beautiful?" I have no idea what I'm capable of or where I can go without doing harm to my balance, but I'm willing to try a whole lot of things if it will let us feel this way again.

Her head tilts in that way she has when she's thinking hard. "Honestly? Maybe not very often."

That's somehow not the answer I expected, and the gorilla jumps around in the back of my head, worried that she's saying it for the wrong reasons.

Her hands rub circles on my chest. Soothing. "You've watched me for months. How often do I play as a Domme?"

My brain manages to find enough neurons to catch up with her question. "Not often. But I thought that was maybe lack of opportunity."

She smiles. "No."

She doesn't say anything more about that, and I don't need her to. It's the truth of Ari that matters right now, not anything else. I run my hands down her arms. "Sore?" I know what mine can feel like after a drum set.

She smiles and hands me the arnica gel. "In a scene, the people participating pick one way to be together. Life isn't like that. So I can't promise my Domme won't sneak out over breakfast sometimes just like my brat does. And sometimes what I really want is cuddly vanilla sex by the fire."

My cock is all about that. Which is crazy. He should be exhausted.

Ari grinds down into me and grins. "We need to stop by the grocery store on the way to your place. Your fridge is down to three carrots and a bottle of ketchup."

I grin and tip my forehead into hers, because that right there just illustrated her point better than anything else. Relationships are living things. They flow, and a lot of things can happen in a river. Including cuff-swapping and emergency grocery runs. "You know it's midnight, right?"

She laughs. "Okay, carrots dipped in ketchup it is."

I just keep rubbing her arms. We'll figure out the food thing just like we're figuring out everything else. By playing with balance and extremes, with standing up and tipping over, with beats that fall where they should and a few that land somewhere else entirely. We don't need to be a Dom and a sub or a Dom and a switch or anything other than Ari and Jackson.

Who might occasionally squabble over who's wearing the cuffs.

"You two done yet?" Scorpio sounds oddly amused, which is the first time since I got naked that I really process how many other people are probably listening. "Because if all you have is carrots at home, you might want to get to this food before Harlan and Quint hog it all."

It takes my eyes a moment to focus on anything beyond Ari's face. When I do, I have to laugh. Every couch and chair in the club has apparently migrated into the dungeon, and there's an impromptu buffet of takeout containers laid out on every reasonably flat surface.

Scorpio grins. "Indian food. Extra spicy."

I've eaten with Scorpio before. If she ordered, nobody in here is going to be able to taste anything tomorrow.

Ari hops off my lap. "Back in a jiffy. Don't move. I'll load us up some plates."

I start to clamber to my feet to head after her, and then I realize why she's really offered. Because there are eyes on me from all over the dungeon—and she trusts me to handle them on my own.

I hide a grin. Apparently it took a turn at being her sub to get rid of her lingering fears that I might be fragile.

I keep my body relaxed, which isn't hard, because the gorilla still has me pretty well pinned. I look around, meeting all the eyes I can see. I'm not naive. I've heard the chatter in the training classes. Quint and Ari sandblast it with quiet, thorough explanations, but there will still be some who don't understand what I did or why. Which I could just shrug off, but I know about villages and the proper sweeping of them. Some things shouldn't get left lying around underfoot.

I see a few faces that have doubts. Some are Dommes from the demo, but I can also see Amelia's eyes tracking ahead of mine, assembling a line-up of who needs to learn to respect submission. Quint is busy multitasking his sub and a takeout container, but Harlan is standing against the side wall, his eyes moving just like Amelia's.

There are lots of people here who understand how to sweep a village.

Tank's eyes just make me want to laugh. The big guy has a look of honest curiosity, and the sub in his lap looks as daunted as I've ever seen her. Ari meets my eyes over Eva's head and grins. Apparently we've started something—and it might be contagious.

I'm good with that. Really good.

Chapter Fifty-Six

ARI

I shake my head at Harlan as I steal food from his container. "Could you be more obvious?"

He raises a confused eyebrow. "What?"

"You're making a list of all the Doms who think a guy might be weak for letting his sub tie him up."

He snorts. "Damn straight. They're idiots, and we do something about that around here."

Yes we do, and I'm usually leading the charge. Tonight, a guy fresh out of training class led it instead. But I know Harlan, and I have no plans to get in his way. I will, however, steal his food and mess with his head. "Scorpio might like tying you up. That would make a pretty clear point."

He shakes his head and grins. "Good try. I already offered and she said no, end of story."

Damn. I missed that one. "There are some others who are curious. I hope you're making that list too."

He rolls his eyes. "Do I look like I just got here yesterday? Go feed your guy. He's let people stare at him long enough."

The eyes in the back of my head know that Jackson is just fine. I'm making this tour for me—and in service of us. I balance two plates that are already well loaded and head for Amelia. She just raises an eyebrow and dares me to stick my chopsticks in her take-out container.

I grin. "Sorry for completely ballsing up your demo."

She chuckles. "You do realize how many switches this is going to pull out of the woodwork, right?"

I shrug casually. "If you want to try being tied up, I'm sure I can find someone who would be gentle with you."

Amelia does lethal better than anyone, but her eyes are way too amused to pull it off. "You've found a good one. Enjoy him."

There are tops who don't respect subs. She's one of the hardest on hers—but she honors what they give her right down to the ground. "Thank you for teaching me how to do it right."

She smiles—and hands me her container. "Go. He's watching you."

I turn, and I can't keep the dopey, stupid grin off my face. I waltz back over and plop in Jackson's lap, and I manage it all without tripping over my suddenly lazy feet or dumping food on either of us.

He laughs and kisses my temple as he takes the plates out of my grip. Then he leans down and casually unzips my boots. "You're drunk, beautiful."

I am. On exactly what he thinks I am. I'm sitting in his lap in my latex pants and my bare feet, surrounded by my tribe. He's naked as a jaybird, his grin is almost as dopey as mine, and he sees every inch of who I am. I'm done holding back and we both know it.

I've found my person.

Chapter Fifty-Seven

EPILOGUE - JACKSON

A lot of things in my life have taken a sharp turn into amazing, but this is one of my favorites. I've been awake for almost half an hour, breathing in the magic of a sunny winter morning in Seattle, stroking the hair of the woman curled up next to me.

I'm sorely tempted to do a lot more than touch her hair, but I've learned from experience that Ari sleeps like the dead. Teasing her awake involves body armor, blunt instruments, and a coffee intravenous drip, not necessarily in that order. Which means I get a lot of mornings like this one, spent in sleepy, cuddly, Ari-appreciating meditation. Quiet time to soak in the epic goodness of having someone in my life who wants to snuggle in this close and stay there.

I know it's only been a few weeks, but I see in Ari what I see in myself. Some of our journeys are long and slow, some are fast and full of lightning—but they're all deep. The measure of what lives between us isn't in the time it's taken to get here.

I kiss her forehead and grin. She's still way deep under, and I don't want to leave this morning without seeing her beautiful blue eyes, even if all she does after that is roll back over and go to sleep. Ari and the crack of dawn do not have a friendly relationship. I'm trying to show her the joys of a good afternoon nap instead, but all that's doing is increasing the amount of time we spend horizontal. Which is not a complaint. At all. Horizontal with Ari is way up at the top of my favorite ways to spend time.

I wait to see if she starts any of the little grunts and wiggles that are the precursors to her waking up in the next hour. I have a rope-bondage lesson with the only other kinky guy in town who gets up before noon on a Saturday, and given how the first one went, I need caffeine on board before I get there. The knots aren't any more complicated than the ones needed to make a drum, but knowing when and where and how and why to use them is, and Matteo is adamant that I learn all of those things before I accost some sub with a rope.

He knows as well as I do that there's only one sub I want to tie up, but I'm trying to keep that a secret, which is why this lesson is going to be happening while all the rest of the kinky people are still snug in their beds. Ari's birthday is in three months, and I have plans.

My gorgeous sloth is definitely not waking up. I start the process of trying to extract myself from underneath her, which my cock totally misunderstands. I chuckle quietly. He's not at all deprived these days, but he's still really unimpressed with the idea of leaving warm, soft, naked woman.

He's got a point.

I grin. I have an idea that might wake her up. One I got consent for long enough ago that she's probably forgotten. I shoot a look down my belly in the direction of my cock. If this backfires, he's going to need to run for cover.

I ease Ari onto her belly and pull her outer knee up. The better to protect my balls.

I reach for the coconut oil that's rapidly replaced lube at my place, and the small, curvy stainless steel toy I stashed in the nether regions of my bedside table for exactly this purpose.

Ari doesn't even twitch when I slide fingers slick with oil over her pussy. I grin again. She might be comatose, but her pussy isn't. It's greeting my fingers with cheerful, wet abandon. I let the slick of her and the oil blend, my fingers traveling her folds, finding all the nerve endings she likes best, giving a happy morning welcome to her clit.

I smile and nuzzle into the woman who still looks sound asleep. Her head might be, but her ass is waking up, with slow, languorous movements that push in the general direction of my hand.

I take my fingers away long enough to grab the vibrator, and then, because I'm a Dom, and one who has to leave in less than an hour, I apply it directly to her clit on maximum power.

Ari doesn't actually manage to shoot off the bed as she wakes up, because I'm smart enough to be lying on top of her, but the sound that comes out of her is a whacked blend of unfiltered fury and high holy pleasure.

I hang on tight, one hand holding her neck down on the bed, the other holding the vibe to her clit. She comes a second time sharply on the heels of the first, her whole body shaking as lightning hits the same place twice.

I toss the vibe away and line up my cock as she finally finds her words.

Her single, whispered word. "Fuck."

Really happy to oblige. I keep my hand on her neck, because I've learned that Ari stays where I put her head, and ram myself into her balls deep.

She lets out a hot, low moan, still heavy with sleep, and I nearly come. Her ass starts to wiggle and plead and I pull almost all the way out before I plunge inside her again.

Ari convulses, another orgasm lashing her hard.

I'm taking notes. She's responsive as fuck when she's half awake.

I lay all my weight on top of her again, holding her down, giving her nowhere to run. Riding the storm with her. Then I reach out for the vibe I threw away and slide it underneath us.

Another short, intense thrust and I stay deep, buried inside her, and land the vibe on her clit. On low this time, but it doesn't matter. She wails into the bright morning sun, the out-of-control cry of a sub who wasn't awake enough to pull her resistance together. She hurtles over the edge she never got to stand on and choose, and I can hear the wild quaking of that inside the storm of her pleasure.

I keep the vibe right where it is. For the first time ever, I'm not asking for her surrender.

I'm taking it.

Her fists clench and she tries to push up, to resist, to move away from the devilish finger of steel assaulting her clit.

I hold firm. I've got her and she knows it and it's time she knows I can take away the last of her shields too.

She melts. There's no other word for it, even as another orgasm crashes over her and pulls me with it. We're riding the crazy arm of the hurricane and she's just gone ragdoll soft underneath me.

I toss the vibe and wrap her as tightly as I can with arms and legs and love and let us shake.

Chapter Fifty-Eight

EPILOGUE - ARI

Only a truly evil Dom would try to make me like mornings.

I manage to drag one eye open, and the first thing I see is the innocent looking oblong hunk of metal that just blitzed my clit. I give it the best glare I can manage before noon. "I'm totally figuring out how to take the batteries out of that thing."

The dead weight on top of me chuckles. "If you do, I'll show you its bigger cousin."

I bury my head in my pillow. Jackson rarely makes threats, but they're never idle. "Sorry, Sir. I'll be very good, I promise."

He swats my hip. "Way too late for that. Pillow under your belly, ass up."

That requires way more energy than I have, especially with a couple hundred pounds of Dom lying on top of me. "Are you sure we can't just lie here and have a nap?" It's a good bribe. He likes naps.

"Nope." He swats me harder this time, and squarely on my ass, which means I no longer have hot guy plastered all over me. "I have to go soon, but first I'm going to lick you until you scream."

Dammit, he knows how to use his carrots and sticks. The man has a really talented tongue.

I reach up a hand and grab a pillow, but that's about as far as I get before there's a strong arm under my hips, dragging me down until my legs are off the end of the bed.

I grin into the blankets. Impatient Dom. One who knows just how much I like sweet post-sex orgasms.

His hand cracks and I gasp as I realize it's my pussy he's just hit and not my ass. Someone's feeling feisty today—and using moves he never would have tried a couple of weeks ago. Pussy spanking doesn't live on the beginner shelf.

I wiggle a tiny bit, hoping for another one.

I get it, but this one is sharp, right to the edge of what still counts as pleasure for me.

My brain stutters. I've gotten my head a whole lot straighter in the past few weeks. It's not the skill I was waiting for. Skills can be learned. It's the bravery. I've always been willing to push myself right to the edge of who I am. I'm not saying that's better or worse than what anyone else does, but it's who I am. I was waiting for the man who could meet me there, who knows where his own bravery lives.

But hot damn, I don't mind these new skills he's growing either.

I shouldn't be surprised. He's moved into the inner sanctum of the Dom ranks faster than any trainee I've ever seen, and while I know it's not because of his skills, the people in those ranks won't let him stay a beginner at anything for long. Not when he's so clearly one of them.

And so clearly mine.

His tongue licks straight up my pussy and then his hand is there again, a sharp, slapping beat as counterpoint to the warm tease of his tongue.

I bury my face in the blankets. This isn't going to be a

sweet orgasm, not even close. I have no idea how I still have one packing a wallop left inside me, but his tongue and his hands are chasing it and nothing inside me is awake enough to stop it.

I snicker and then groan as his wicked, talented tongue circles my clit. I don't need to stop this orgasm or any other ones, and my Dom can be as evil as he wants. I always have the option to get even. I make a mental note to scoop up that vibe when we're done, and then I'm done making mental notes. I'm gripping the covers in a desperate effort to hold still as his tongue wreaks havoc. I know what happens if I move, and it isn't a pussy spanking. He likes his drums stationary.

He chases me right to half a breath before I go over—and then he stops the madness. His tongue glides, soft and slow in my folds as he hums into my most sensitive parts, singing some kind of gentle, ticklish lullaby to my marshmallow.

I feel the giggles rising up, and the softness. Always, the softness. He calls it out of me effortlessly now, stretching me out and spinning me full of air and light until softness is all of who I am.

Maybe mornings are redeemable.

LOVE: A FETTERED VALENTINE

(as told by Ari)

That's the end of NEED, but Ari thinks you should all come to the Fettered Valentine's Day party. Consider it a series finale, or an order from your favorite switch, whichever you prefer. ;)

————

People keep saying there's something in the pink drinks. There must be, and the evidence has never been more obvious than it is today.

I grin at the shiny pink streamers overhead. If you don't look too closely, they're covered in cute purple hearts. If you look closely, and most people are, they're cute kinky purple hearts, alterations hand drawn by Sam and his minions and festooned all over the club in a stealth brat mission early this morning.

I, however, was not allowed to take part. Sam himself ushered me straight out the front door about ten seconds after I arrived. Apparently we weren't the only ones invading the club at the crack of dawn.

I could have put the pieces together. My Dom's favorite

travel mug abandoned on the bar. The truck belonging to Matteo, the king of rope bondage, parked half a block away. The furtive glances every sub who was there this morning casts my way every time someone mentions my birthday.

I could have put the pieces together—but I won't.

Sometimes life is better if you let it surprise you.

I look around at one of my favorite places in the world, filled with most of the people I love, and let myself glow like a light bulb. Fettered's Valentine's Day party might be my favorite one all year, because I'm a kinky romantic and everyone knows it. On this day, I get to be a very public marshmallow all day long.

I look over at where my guy is sitting on his stool, tapping out the rhythms of this night, and grin. He woke me up again this morning. He takes his life into his own hands every time he does it, because I don't always wake up in a submissive mood—but I always love where we end up.

I hope he does it again soon. Right after the brand new tattoo on my ass is all healed up.

Jackson winks at me, but his face disappears as Damon crosses between us, Emily tucked in at his side. She's wearing a brand-new yellow sundress, faithfully modeled on the old one. Chloe made her three of them because Emily's Dom lacks control where yellow is concerned. This one is silk, and it's gorgeous, and only Emily could pull off a shiny yellow sundress at a kink club in the middle of February.

Although I'm not sure her Dom is going to let her keep wearing it. He's got a look in his eye.

Sam slides up beside me, and I blink. Hard. He's got Soleil in his arms. We can have kids and babies in here when the events are non-alcoholic, and this one is, but still. I figured she'd be tucked at home with the puppy I helped her get her daddies for Valentine's Day.

Then I see Evie dash through some legs behind him and I know something's up. I give Sam a look. "What's going on?"

He shakes his head. "I don't know. Damon called and said to be here and to bring the kids."

My head swivels to follow my boss, who's walking toward the stage.

Damon says a few words into Scorpio's ear and takes her microphone. She gives it up without a fight, which means she can smell whatever just hit the airwaves too. Damon clears his throat and the club silences, except for Evie, who takes another few steps before she realizes nobody else is making noise anymore. Jimmy scoops her up and sits her on his shoulders, and all eyes are facing forward.

Damon clears his throat again, and I can practically feel his nerves. Obviously Emily can too, because she lifts a hand to his chest. Soothing her Dom, even if she has no idea why he's nervy.

He settles the hand holding the mike on top of hers. "Everyone here knows that the amazing woman in my life plans a really great party."

Nobody so much as breathes. We know better than to interrupt a scene.

He smiles. "I didn't want her to plan this one." He turns to face Emily and drops to one knee. "Marry me, sweetheart."

Her eyes get as big as eyes can go.

Sam is a pillar of shocked joy beside me, and he's not alone.

Damon chuckles and kisses Emily's hand. "Let's do this today, love. Here, where it all started."

In a beautiful silk version of her yellow sundress. I close my eyes in a quick nod to the boss man's moves. We all missed today's most stealth mission of all.

Emily has no words, but nobody needs them. Consent is written in her tears, in the blinding happiness of her smile, in the shaking of every part of her as Damon scoops her up and hugs her in tight.

We get about three seconds to melt into kinky goo and then Scorpio takes her microphone back. She looks over at Damon and gives him the evil eye. "You might think we can't plan a wedding on two minutes' notice, but you would be wrong." She looks out at the audience. "Sam, make us an aisle. Band guys, figure out what the heck we're playing. Chloe, flowers and something to tie them up with."

Chloe flashes her a huge grin, pulls a streamer remnant out of her pocket, and starts plucking flowers out of the arrangements on the buffet table. Sam looks at me, eyes wide and panicked and full of glee. "The yellow ribbons and candles and bowls from when they did their first scene together. Where are they?"

The man is freaking brilliant. I grab Mattie, who's charging our way, and shove us all in the direction of the back closet where we keep strange shit. It's all in a box, hoping they might want it again some day. This wasn't what I imagined when I packaged it up, but I just won the award for world's best packrat.

It takes us four minutes.

Four. Minutes.

Because that's all we need, and because that's all the time Damon is willing to give us.

In four minutes, we have Emily ready at the entrance to the lounge, her bare feet standing at the beginning of a gorgeous aisle of yellow ribbons and candles. We have a band ready to play whatever four rock-and-roll kinksters could come up with on short notice. Gabby has even managed to turn a bunch of the treats that used to be spread out on the tables into a stack of goodies that resembles a wedding cake. Evie and Tash are ready to jump out of their skins at their new job, and someone has quietly disappeared the flower carcasses that gave up their petals to be thrown wherever two little girls decide to throw them. Daniel is standing at the front, looking sheepish and proud and apparently ordained enough to officiate at a wedding.

And every heart in this place is ready to burst.

Damon has the mike again, and this time, there is no throat clearing. His eyes are glued to Emily, but he speaks to all of us. "This is our wedding, but we started here with all of you around us, and I hope we continue that way. If anyone else wants to promise to have and to hold and to sometimes tie up, or to renew those promises, the woman who is about to be my wife would like to invite you to stand up and join us." He grins and finally looks out at all of us. "Apparently she had to plan something."

There's laughter in response, and teasing—and there's movement. Other couples finding each other, some with sweetness, some with raised eyebrows, some with an ass swat or two to hurry things along. I grin as Sam and Leo lean together with Soleil squished between them. Grin harder as Daniel gets joined by his sub. Those two have a wedding date set in six months, but it looks like they might be getting in a practice session. But it's Scorpio who makes me grin hardest, backing away from Harlan with utter panic in her eyes and yes on her lips.

I finally just let my grin take over my face, because the awesomeness has no end. I see Quint and Meghan, both shaking their heads and laughing and hopping up to sit on the bar for a really good view. Eva and Tank, looking terrified and glowing like sunbeams. Doxie, quietly cuddled in to Jimmy, gazing out in soft delight on what the two of them started. Mattie and Milo haven't gone anywhere, but I know as soon as

I see their joined hands over her belly that this day isn't done handing out its surprises yet.

An arm slides around my waist. "I know we aren't making lifelong promises quite yet, but will you come sit in my lap while I play the drums?"

I close my eyes. I should have gone to him. I suddenly wish, with all my heart, that I had.

His fingers turn my chin to face him. "No way, beautiful. Don't you dare apologize. We're exactly perfect right where we're at and I'm not looking to speed anything up." He kisses me, soft as butterfly wings. "But maybe if we sit close enough to the action, it will be contagious."

I close my eyes, lean in, and tell my immune system to go take a nap.

I'm pretty sure I feel a sneeze coming on.

———

(THE END.)

Ari: *Hey, nice people. I told you I'd be back.*

Sam: *Wait another minute or two, sugar. They're still high on wedding fumes.*

Ari: *That's the best time to tell them to buy the next book. Because they really should. It's full of Matteo's rope tricks and hot sex and Lilia wrote the best person for him. I love Liane! I also love India. And Daley. Artists make really amazing kinky people. This is going to be a fab trilogy.*

Sam: *I love that she named a kitten Trouble instead of me.*

Ari: *Ha. Twisted Strands, everyone. In which the most trouble-some character isn't a person named Sam. Preorder here. (Go to www.liliamoon.com if you can't follow links from here.)*

Sam: *Some of them might like to wait.*

Ari: *In that case, they should sign up for Lilia's email list. Because* *after this trilogy there will be my new series. And Jackson's. And some cows, because apparently I've lost my ever-loving mind.*

Sam: *Focus, sugar. Preorder or email list, sexy reader people. Pick one.*

Ari: *Lilia wants us to give choices.*

Sam: *We did. We gave them two.*

Ari: *Some of them might want to wait and catch it later when they're browsing for books.*

Sam: *Seriously? That's how you miss out on the good stuff, people. Don't listen to her.*

Ari: *Freely given consent, Sam.*

Sam: *They will miss out on spankings. And adorable Soleil sightings. And what happens when an idiot Dom tries to put a kitten in a canoe.*

Ari: *Sam. Spoilers.*

Leo: *Sam.*

Sam: *Oh, shit.*

.

Printed in Great Britain
by Amazon